THE CHRISTMAS CHRONICLES

THE

Christmas Chronicles

The Legend of Santa Claus

A Novel

TIM SLOVER

BANTAM BOOKS

NEW YORK

Published in the United States by Bantam Books,
an imprint of The Random House Publishing Group,
a division of Random House, Inc., New York.

BANTAM BOOKS is a registered trademark of Random House, Inc.,
and the colophon is a trademark of Random House, Inc.

LIBRARY OF CONGRESS CATALOGING-IN-PUBLICATION DATA
Slover, Tim.
The Christmas chronicles : the legend of Santa Claus, a novel / Tim Slover.
p. cm.
ISBN 978-0-553-80810-0
eBook ISBN 978-0-553-90800-8
1. Santa Claus—Fiction. 2. Christmas stories. I. Title.
PS3569.L6985C48 2010
813'.54—dc22   2010010577

Printed in the United States of America on acid-free paper

www.bantamdell.com

FIRST EDITION

2 4 6 8 9 7 5 3 1

Book design by Dana Leigh Blanchette

Contents

THE CHRISTMAS CHRONICLES

Pine Boughs

I could clearly hear the sound, even through the raucous wind that had suddenly kicked up. But it didn't make any sense, and I couldn't see what was making it. I had thought I was alone on that wintry mountain. Apparently I was wrong. The sunset was just beginning to paint the snow gold, and coming up over a gilded rise, through a stand of swaying white pine, was this *sound*. So I wasn't alone. Someone—or something—was approaching, fast. And, to my complete astonishment, that something was making the unmistakable sound of—

But I'm getting ahead of myself. I want to tell what happened precisely and in the right order. That way you'll have the best chance to make up your mind about it. Because, make no mistake, that's what you're being called on to do here: decide. Once you know what I now know, you're going to have to figure out what to do about it. If you don't feel up to that task, well, you might want to stop reading right now. But I wouldn't. Knowledge is responsibility, all right, but in this case, if you let it, it can also be sheer delight.

The events happened last year, in that magical, occasionally peaceful, usually mad-dash season between Thanksgiving and Christmas. Despite our fervent September resolutions, late November found all of us without our Christmas shopping, Christmas decorating, Christmas cards, or Christmas baking done. Or, actually, started. But the first skiff of snow had just come to the particular valley of the Rocky Mountains where we live—my wife and I and our two teenaged sons—and we were all in love with the new weather. We felt energized and ready to plunge into Christmas toils.

"I love the first snow," my wife said happily. "It makes

such a nice change." The boys agreed. I saw my opportunity.

"Who wants to drive up the mountain and cut pine boughs?" I asked. A certain disheartening silence greeted my invitation, a pause while all three invented their plausible excuses. The wife spoke vaguely of golf clubs in need of polishing. A boy had a girlfriend to see. Another boy had to meet up with his band.

"But we need pine boughs," I objected. "What about the Advent wreath? What about branches for decorating the front door? And the mantel? And the stair railing?"

"You get them, honey," my wife said. "You're the one who really loves getting the car stuck, slogging through snow, and committing theft on federal land."

It was hard to argue with that. So, without accompaniment, I pulled on a pair of pack boots, grabbed some gardening gloves and lopping shears, and drove the car clear out of town up into the mountains, following my usual route. Just me and an MP3 full of Christmas music.

Usually I drive until the road—which is never plowed—gets too slippery and snow-packed for my old car to keep going safely. Then I drive about a quarter mile farther—just because it's so fun to drive on slippery snowpack—until it's definitely too dangerous to go on. And then I go about another hundred yards and, if I haven't gotten stuck by then, park on the shoulder of the road. I hike and scramble up into the trees until I strike an area isolated enough that even the most overzealous ranger would be unlikely to venture. Then I trudge around cutting until I have about twenty boughs of white pine and Douglas fir and drag them back to the car. The whole thing usually takes a couple of hours.

Remember, the snow came late on this particular year. That meant the car could go farther than usual before the road got too dangerous. Before long I was up higher than I had ever been. I found myself driving on a ridge with tall fir and bare white aspen pressing close on both sides of the road. On an impulse I rolled down the window—I don't know why, maybe to see the trees without a pane of glass between us. The cold air that rushed in was unusual. It seemed to effervesce like soda water, as though every molecule were dancing. In fact, everything on that ridge seemed so alive that I had a strong impulse to sing a Christmas carol to the trees as I drove along. But the truth is, if you start singing to trees, you risk them singing back. And then you have to reassess your whole system of thought. So though I was tempted, I refrained.

But when you're distracted by fizzy air and potentially musical trees, it's not surprising that your driving might suffer. Before I knew it I hit a patch of ice, swerved to the right, and skidded to a halt. I climbed out of the car, now distinctly listing toward the passenger side, and groaned at the sight that met my eyes: The car was up to its wheel wells, two of which were in the ditch running down from the shoulder of the road, in snow. The car was well and truly stuck as it had never been stuck before, and it obviously wasn't going to get unstuck on its own steam, or mine. It was tow-truck stuck. On a very isolated road, well out of cellphone range. And with the sun riding down the sky toward setting. I would have to walk back down the road until I got a signal to call for help.

And that's when I got the idea that led to everything else. A higher hill crowned with white pine reared up from the other side of the ditch. *Don't trek back down the road,* I thought; *climb up the ridge and see what you can see. And, as a bonus, you'll get a strong signal for your cellphone, and you can make your call and get rescued.* I didn't question the impulse; I just started hiking.

Once I got to the crest of the hill, I knew I'd made the right decision. I looked out and saw an amazing sight. To the west, the sun was now dipping toward the horizon, bathing everything in that rich amber light that sometimes comes at sunset. But in the east gray clouds, heavy with snow, were rolling down from the top of the mountain. A wind came up, first stirring and then toss-ing the boughs of the trees on the hill. I stood stock-still. It was a scene of utter enchantment: the golden sunlight streaming from the west, the dense clouds blowing down from the east, the roar of the wind, the glad, dancing trees. I got the powerful feeling that when those clouds met that sunlight, which would be happening in a moment right where I was standing, anything, absolutely anything, might happen.

That's when I heard the sound. It was rhythmic, silvery: jing, jing, JING! jing, jing, JING! And it was coming up on me fast over the slope, just as the snow clouds were rolling down from the mountain.

Jing, jing, JING! jing, jing, JING! And now the clouds were upon me, and with them the snow: big white flakes blowing in with the wind. And when the gray clouds and swirling snow met that amber sunlight, the scene instanta-neously transformed. Gold lit up the clouds like a flashlight shining through tissue paper, and turned each snowflake into a dancing firefly. Every pine needle and bare aspen twig was sharp and clear. The snow on the ground was a dazzling carpet of fiery diamonds. I could have stared at it all for hours.

But I didn't get the chance. Because now the jing, jing, JING! was actually upon me. And at last I could see what was making the sound. It was merry, silver harness bells! And the harness was around the neck of—

You will hardly believe me; you will think I'm making up a story. Well, all right, yes, I have been known to make up a story or two, but this isn't one of them. What I'm telling you is the simple truth. The harness bells were around the neck of a small reindeer with graceful two-point antlers. And the reindeer's coat glowed red—not orange, which is what we usually mean when we say hair or fur is red—but actually deep, vivid scarlet. I didn't learn until later that I was in the presence of a legend.

The crimson reindeer was pulling a swift, light sleigh, which dodged through the trees on its silver runners with great nimbleness and speed. I only caught a glimpse of its driver, but he looked like a perfectly ordinary young man, except that he, like the reindeer, seemed to give off a faint light of his own. He held no reins. He simply clutched the bench where he sat as the sleigh raced on. His expression, if I read it right in the split second I saw it, was one of worry and dread. "Hurry!" I heard him say. "It's right behind us! And you know they can't anchor the Road for more than a moment!"

In response the reindeer replied fiercely—

But no, how can I report to you what a reindeer said? You won't believe me. You may already be wondering if I was drunk up on that mountain, or deranged. Well, I'm pleased to report that I have never taken a drop stronger than eggnog in my life and have passed every magazine mental acuity test my wife has given me. With flying colors. So you must make of it what you will when I tell you that the reindeer replied, and he panted as he said it, "I would . . . rather stand and fight . . . Professor Wyatt!"

"No!" cried the Professor, and he seemed very alarmed. "Not this time! We're wanted at the castle!"

Then the sleigh flashed past. I spun around to watch it go. I'm sure neither man nor beast saw me. But as they drove with single-minded concentration, not two yards away from me, they suddenly made a sharp left turn, too sharp, trying to get onto—

Look. I'm going to be revealing so many wonders over the course of this account that you might just as well get used to contemplating them. I've had to. So I shall stop hesitating and trying to prepare you for the incredible. I'll just assume you're keeping up.

They were trying to get onto a road that a moment before did not exist. At least I had not seen it. Of course, I was intent on looking at snowflakes and scarlet reindeer, so I might have missed it. It might have been there all along. But I don't think so. I believe it appeared just as this Professor Wyatt and the reindeer were trying to enter it.

The road was very steep, about twenty feet wide, made of a single sheet of white ice as smooth as a mirror, and led up about thirty yards directly into the swirl of cloud and light overhead. At its foot were two neatly trimmed variegated holly bushes in brightly polished silver pots, one on each side of the road. On each pot was etched a reindeer rampant and a star. The scent of peppermint wafted from the holly, and inhaling it, I felt as though I wanted to run a marathon and then swim the Pacific Ocean.

Meanwhile the sleigh was trying desperately to get onto the road, but was approaching it at too acute an angle.

"Look out!" shouted Professor Wyatt. "You're missing the entrance! We'll be stranded!"

"I know . . . what I'm . . . doing!" panted the reindeer.

And he did. He gritted his teeth, got a hoof between the holly bushes, pivoted smartly on it, and swung into the road. The sleigh careened wide behind the reindeer, a runner came off the ground, sliced off a sprig of the left-hand bush without knocking over its pot, and then both runners slammed down onto the road as the reindeer bounded up its steep, shining slope. That jolt sent a Something bouncing out of the sleigh and onto the road. It was solid and heavy and very close to the dimensions of the *Oxford English Dictionary, Compact Edition*. It slid down eleven feet of road, and stopped almost right at my feet.

"Well done!" shouted the Professor as they disappeared up the road into the clouds and out of sight. Neither man nor beast noticed that the Something had fallen from their sleigh.

The moment they were gone, the road began to lose its solidity. For an instant it flickered like a fluorescent light struggling to come on, and then it winked out and was gone. And so were the holly bushes, except for the one sprig. Now everything changed back in an instant. The extraordinary light dimmed as the sun slipped below the western horizon. The snow stopped falling. The air grew chill, and I zipped my coat up to my throat. I suddenly felt weary, drained by what I had just witnessed. Automatically, I hauled out my cellphone to see if I had a signal. I didn't.

And then, before I even had time to think of what to do next, it was on top of me.

Even now, from a comforting distance in time, as I contemplate what happened next it makes me shudder. What I can only describe as a grayness came rushing up to me, flying over the same path the sleigh had just run. It had edges, this grayness, and its shape was a roiling, churning storm cloud with a vortex at its center.

In a moment it was upon me, and I found myself engulfed in clammy coldness. I could still see the world from inside the gray cloud, but everything I looked at was drained of all color and life. It was hard to breathe, an exertion just to keep my heart beating. And just as the grayness sapped the world of color, so it bled it dry of hope. When I tried to think of good things, they all seemed mockeries. And I found I couldn't believe in anything. I doubted now I had just seen a sleigh and a road. Did my wife love me? Was Christmas coming, and after it a new year to look forward to? No. The future was a bleak and featureless misery, as far as my mind could look ahead. And in a moment, I lost the ability even to do that. There was no future, no past, just the endless depressing torment of the gray present. And then, most horrible of all, I found myself unable even to believe that anything existed outside the shape that engulfed me. It wasn't a shape at all, really; it was the whole world, the universe, all there was.

I now believe there is something worse than dying. It is hopelessness. Because complete and utter hopelessness makes you want to die, and that must be worse than dying. I sank to my knees and then fell on my face, sightless, filled to the brim with despair and ready to give in.

But then, not quite sightless. By luck, if you believe in such ideas, I had fallen in view of the Something that had dropped from the sleigh. The overpowering grayness had come so quickly after it had slid to my feet that I had forgotten it. Now there it lay, along with the sprig of holly still giving off its faint whiff of peppermint.

It was the peppermint that saved me. It cleared my head a little and lessened the grip of the cloud. I clutched the holly and brought it close to my face, breathing in its fragrance. That gave me the strength to reach out for the Something. It was a large, leather-bound green book in a matching slipcase. And as my fingers touched its pebbly texture, the grayness left me. Despair left me, too, melting away as a nightmare does in morning sunlight. Hope seeped back in. Of course: Christmas was coming. And New Year's after that. And as for my wife, she loved me even after I made caramel apples on the couch last Halloween while I was watching a football game.

As for the gray cloud, it rushed on. I was not its object, after all. Though it had felt like an eternity, all that it had made me feel had happened in a few moments as it passed over me. Its real purpose was to get onto the road before it entirely disappeared.

But it was too late. The road was gone. The way was shut. It threw itself against the clouds, but they were to it a stone wall, and it banged against them with a horrible shriek of rage and despair. Then it shot away over the horizon as fast as it had come. A roll of thunder came from where it disappeared.

I hugged the heavy green book to my chest as I climbed down the bank back to where my car was. I found I was shaking and had to move slowly and carefully to keep from slipping in the snow. My plan now was to stow the book in the car, take a few deep, steadying breaths, and then walk back down the road to get into cellphone range.

But I found I didn't have to. There was the car, out of the ditch and even turned the right way to drive back down the mountain. I took the steadying breaths anyway. A spicy scent made me open the lid of the trunk. There were pine boughs in there, tied neatly together at the stems with silver ribbon. A small card printed in green ink placed on top of them read, "Merry Christmas."

There was no one home when I got there, and that was fine with me. Much had happened that I didn't understand, and I wasn't ready to talk about it to anyone. Perhaps the book would provide some kind of explanation. I took it into my study and examined it.

It was large and beautiful, bound in forest green leather covers, with sewn signatures, thick, creamy paper, and three attached silk bookmarks. The only unfortunate thing about it was that it was unreadable. At least by me. The text was filled with umlauts and accent marks and long words with a sprinkling of strange letters. I took it this was German or Welsh or some Scandinavian language, but I wasn't really sure. Whatever it was, I couldn't read it.

I flipped through the pages. Many were filled with graphs and tables that seemed to indicate production over time of various items. One page, which folded out, seemed to be a contract of some sort, complete with a red wax seal. Several more were devoted to detailed maps of various parts of the world, showing what I took to be wind currents marked out. The first part of the book, however, was of a different character. It appeared to be a story or history. There were engravings in this section: a boy making a wooden chair, a merry girl sewing a coat, a bearded man with his arm around the neck of a reindeer, a grave council sitting around a large table.

I flipped back to what was clearly the title page and saw what I had missed before: an engraving of a thumbprint in the lower right-hand corner.

Now it occurred to me that given the events of the day, if I pressed my thumb onto that print, something extraordinary was likely to happen. I would be plunged deeper into an adventure that was already threatening to overturn my cherished notions of reality. So perhaps I can be forgiven if I hesitated. I shut the book and left the study. I wandered into the kitchen. I ate chips and salsa. I watched the news on TV. That last activity was all it took to make up my mind.

I returned to the study, opened the book to the title page, and placed my thumb firmly on the print. A mild vibration and a warm sensation entered my hand, stayed there for a few moments, and then left. And then the words on the title page formed themselves into something I could read. As simple as that. It was as though the book learned who I was from my thumbprint and adjusted its language accordingly.

The title page read as follows:

The Green Book

**Being the True and Authorized Chronicle of Klaus,
Sometimes Styled Father Christmas, Père Noël,
Santa Claus, and Sundry Other Names
Including, Wrongly,
Saint Nicholas.**

Also a Record of Important Recent Events
of the Last Few Centuries
at Castle Noël in the True North
Together with Production Figures and
an Almanac of Christmas Flights

WRITTEN AND COMPILED BY

DUNSTAN WYATT, ES

COURT HISTORIAN

I sat back to assess. Apparently I had in my possession what purported to be a biography of someone who doesn't exist. I had believed in Santa Claus when I was a child, given him up reluctantly when the laughter of other children had proved too strong, and then disregarded him altogether. Santa Claus was made up. Santa Claus was just a way for malls to get parents to buy more than they could afford. Santa Claus was, as my boys would say, extremely over.

But the reindeer, the sleigh, the road, the early Christmas present of pine boughs and a dislodged car? And the author, "Dunstan Wyatt, ES"—whatever that meant: Surely he was the Professor Wyatt who had been on the sleigh? As I thought about these things, something deep within me, something long pent up and dammed, broke loose. I think it was Desire.

So I started to read *The Green Book*. I read it all night in my study. I fell asleep around dawn after I finished it. When I woke up, I intended to go straight into the bedroom, tell my wife all about what had happened, and show her the book. But the book was gone. In its place was a handwritten note:

"We needed this back," it said. "But don't worry; you'll remember every word. Tell the world, before it's too late, when and if you feel brave enough. Yours sincerely, Dunstan."

I think I feel brave enough. Do you? Because I did remember every word of Professor Wyatt's book, and what follows is his account, revealed to the world now for the first time. Are you ready? You are about to read the true history of Santa Claus.

The True and Authorized Chronicle of Santa Claus

(from The Green Book)

WRITTEN FROM ORIGINAL SOURCES AND INTERVIEWS

BY PROFESSOR DUNSTAN WYATT, ES,

COURT HISTORIAN, CASTLE NOËL

Author's Note: *Welcome, Esteemed Reader. While a biography of this brief length cannot make a claim to completeness, it does to accuracy. It is hoped that this account will correct some misconceptions about its remarkable subject, and, even more important, cheer hearts and open minds. To that end, it is recommended that it be read each and every year at Christmas, silently or aloud, with a mug of hot chocolate ready to hand.*

D.W.

CHAPTER ONE

Klaus the Carpenter

The man whom legend calls Santa Claus was born simply Klaus. He was the first and only child of a skilled carpenter and his good wife, both of whom, I am sorry to say, died when the Black Death came to their village at the foot of Mount Feldberg in the Black Forest in 1343. Little Klaus, barely out of babyhood then, had no other family, and so he was adopted by the Worshipful Guild of Foresters, Carpenters, and Woodworkers. It was very unusual for the Guild to adopt a child, but Klaus's father had been a much-loved member, and so they did it. Of course, the Masters of the Guild were extremely preoccupied with their work of making plows and houses and clock gears—many, many things were made of wood in those days—and they really did not have the time to rear Klaus. So, mostly, they didn't. They gave him plenty of food, which he liked very much. They gave him old carpenter's tools instead of toys. And they gave him genial, distracted pats on the head whenever he came within range—benign neglect. It was a very satisfactory arrangement.

It is not surprising that Klaus became a very fine worker of wood. He had the best carvers and joiners and carpenters to watch and learn from, even though they did not actually notice they were teaching him. What was surprising—even alarming to some in the Guild—was that by the age of seventeen he had quietly surpassed them all. The piece he made to prove that he deserved to be awarded the title Master—his master-piece—was an exceptionally lovely chair by any standard. It was expertly joined, intricately and richly carved, and inlaid with all fourteen hardwoods that grew on Mount Feldberg. It was immediately adopted by the Guild as the new Governor's chair. Klaus was given his Master Woodworker's badge—

a gold pine tree—toasted with ale, and slapped on the back for congratulations.

"We must have raised you well, Klaus," the Masters said, "though we confess we didn't notice."

"Yes, you must have!" said Klaus and laughed. And all the Guild members present at his pinning ceremony joined in the laughter. And that was not surprising, because of the three extraordinary features of Klaus's extraordinary laugh. First, it was exceptionally loud and deep, even when he was a boy, coming from the very roots of his soul. Second, it was completely untainted by any sort of meanness— Klaus never laughed *at* anyone, always *with* them. And third, it tended to make whoever heard it start laughing, too. So, of course, everyone laughed now.

Almost everyone. There was one member who did not laugh. His name was Rolf Eckhof, and he was as thin and hard as an iron spike, with white-blond hair and a pursed mouth that looked as if it could never laugh. And though he was a competent woodsman with commissions enough for common items, he had been trying and failing to become a Master for six years. Now this laughing, carefree boy had done it on his first try—the youngest Master in the history of the Guild.

"But he is just a boy!" Rolf Eckhof sneered.

"Yes, he's *our* boy!" the Masters replied proudly. And they laughed and toasted and congratulated Klaus and themselves all over again.

Rolf Eckhof looked on Klaus's masterpiece and knew he could never make such a beautiful, clever thing. And that knowledge filled him with jealousy and hatred. But he was the sort of man who could wait to take revenge. For now, he said nothing further. But he did not slap Klaus's back, he did not toast him with ale, and certainly he did not laugh.

Klaus did not notice. And if he had, he would not have comprehended. His nature was open and magnanimous. If ever Jupiter predominated in a personality, it did in his: Klaus was, in every sense of the word, Jovial.

And so Klaus built himself a small cottage on the hill above the village and set up on his own as a carpenter and joiner and, especially, wood carver. It was soon well known that if you wanted something special—a stool with legs carved to look like those of a bear or a bridal bed with a headboard inlaid with scenes from the Black Forest—you went to Klaus. And so he prospered. He grew never tall, but deep-chested and very strong, and his hair and beard, when it came in, were the color of a fox's pelt.

But during the summer when Klaus was twenty, something happened that made him stop his fancy carving. The Black Death returned to his village. It did not tarry at his snug cottage, but many another house was visited. The villagers tasted death all that summer and fall and into the winter. Not until the midwinter wind blew down the lanes and snow covered thatch and stone did the Black Death walk on and leave the village in peace. As it happened— and this is one of those quirks a historian finds hard to explain—it never returned.

But it had turned the village into a Swiss cheese, with holes in most families. Here a father was taken and no one else in the household even sickened; there all but one died, a child of three, leaving her to be adopted by a childless aunt. Indeed, all the twenty-seven children who lost parents in that terrible year found homes of some sort, and none wandered alone; that is how the village was. Many went on to become replacement sisters or brothers, daughters or sons, to those who had lost them.

All this Klaus saw, and it wrung his heart. But then a splendid new idea occurred to him. It did not make him laugh, for it was not a time for laughing, but a smile creased his ruddy face and a sparkle came into his hazel eyes.

The next morning he put all his tools into a large flour sack, flung it over his shoulder, and made his way down the hill from his cottage. At the very first house he came to, a small place under a great larch tree, he knocked on the door. A sad-eyed woman holding a baby on her hip answered. "Dame Grusha," said Klaus. "What have you lost?"

Dame Grusha bit her lip. "I have lost my Jacob," she said.

He took her small hands in his red, calloused ones. "I am so sorry, Dame Grusha," he said. "I cannot help that. But"—he let go of her hands and heaved his great sack down onto the cold ground in front of her door; it opened, and she could see the tools inside—"what have you lost that these can replace?"

"I have no table. We burned it because Father Goswin thought it was plague-tainted."

"Let's go inside and measure," said Klaus.

For the next months Klaus scarcely saw his own cottage. He spent all his days in the houses of the village, making and mending, or going to the forest for wood and hauling it back. Door to door he went, and always he asked the same question: "What have you lost?" And he heard the same heartrending answers: "I have lost my Johann," "my Gretchen," "my little Conrad," "all my children," "my old father," "everyone but me."

What could he say to such losses? Only that he was sorry. But what could he do for those who were suffering? A little, he thought, and he did it.

He made chairs and butter churns and many tables, for many had been burned, like Dame Grusha's, after the sick and dying had lain on them. Soon all in the village were familiar with the sight of the strong young man with flaming red hair and beard coming and going, his sack of tools slung over his back; and all knew his question by heart: "What have you lost that I can replace?"

He did not think to charge money for his labors, but he ate and slept wherever he worked, and, despite their grief, or perhaps in relief of it, the villagers liked to tease him for his hearty appetite. "You'll grow fat if you keep eating like that," they jested.

"So be it!" Klaus answered back. "If that is the price I must pay for this good goose, then I say, so be it!" And though he didn't laugh because it wasn't a time yet for laughter, he would smile, and the villagers loved to see his smile in this time of mourning, because they knew it sprang from a heart that wanted only to do them good. It was simple: Klaus knew what to do, and the doing of it made him happy. And all the villagers looked out for him as he stumped down the lanes and across the fields with his flour sack filled with tools, and took a measure of comfort just from seeing him.

But one in the village did not. "He charges nothing for his labors!" Rolf Eckhof complained to the Governor of the Worshipful Guild of Foresters, Carpenters, and Woodworkers. "And nothing for materials! And this at a time when good business practice dictates we should set our prices higher because of the demand! You must do something! Else he will ruin us all!"

But the Governor only fixed Rolf Eckhof with a baleful eye. "For shame," he said. And indeed Rolf Eckhof felt a hot streak of shame run through him, and this, too, he blamed on Klaus. But, remember, he was the sort of man who could wait to take his revenge.

Klaus knew nothing of this. Instead, he brooded on another problem. There were fifty-two surviving children in the village under Mount Feldberg, and Klaus knew them all because he had made and mended in virtually every house. The Black Death had bitten deeper into their lives than those of the grown-ups because they had lived fewer years. They were sadder and quieter than children ought to be, and this troubled Klaus a great deal. Perhaps if they had something to do, he thought—for doing is what had helped to mend his heart. So he engaged as many as he could in his labors, teaching them simple woodworking skills. (And this, Rolf Eckhof would have said, had he known of it, was completely contrary to Guild laws.) And when a child grew too quiet and stared out into nothing for too long, and Klaus knew she was thinking of a lost mother or brother, he would say to her, "Will you go down to the millstream and cut rushes with me? We need them for the Linders' new roof." He could not mend their losses, but he could teach them to help, and the helping, he knew, would go a measure to healing them. And so, in this way, many of the children grew to be really quite useful in bringing the village back to life. And children who did not at first help saw that those who did were happier, and that grown-ups treated them with the respect accorded to all who help, young or old, and so they began to help, too. And then even those who did no work at all claimed they did, and so everyone was included. And the houses went up, and spirits lifted, and the golden days of September saw a better harvest than anyone had expected.

And that is when Klaus had another idea: a novel idea; a truly sensational, momentous Idea. It seemed to travel up from his toes and fill his body inch by upward inch until it came right up into his throat, and he laughed out loud—

the first anyone had laughed for months and months. "Ha, ha, ha!" he laughed. "Ho, ho, ho!" And those who heard that laugh—which was most of the village because of how tremendously loud it was—stopped their raking or bread making, or sprang up from where they had been dozing in the afternoon sun, and smiled. And in that moment, though they were ever sad for their losses, the Black Death well and truly left the hearts of those who lived in the village under Mount Feldberg.

Klaus kept his sensational idea quiet. But the villagers noticed that he did not go out of his house nearly so much as October gave way to November. And when the snow began to fly in December, Klaus loaded his large flour sack—the very one in which he had packed his tools around town—and made his way to the fine stone church in the middle of the village to see the parish priest, Father Goswin.

"I'm not sure that I entirely understand," said Father Goswin when Klaus took an object from the sack and showed it to him. It was a carved wooden bear with legs that really moved.

"It's a toy!" Klaus said proudly. "I have fifty-three! Not all bears, of course." He rummaged around in his sack, filled with the toys he had been making almost without stopping to sleep or eat for the past weeks. "Look at this one! I've made fifteen of these!" He put into Father Goswin's hand a spinning top made of white ash. The priest turned it over in his hand; he could make nothing of it.

"Here," said Klaus. "You have to apply the string." And he wound up the top and sent it skipping and whistling up the nave. It crashed merrily into the choir screen.

"Klaus!" cried Father Goswin in alarm.

"Fifty-three!" said Klaus again, retrieving his top. "Just the number of children in the village, if you count little Lena born last week. Look! I made this for her." Rummaging around in his sack again, he produced a minuscule rattle and shook it. "I mean to take them to all the children's houses!"

"Ah," Father Goswin said. "Why?"

"They have lost so much this year. And then they helped when I needed it. It's their reward!" And at the thought of the children opening their doors and tripping sleepily over a bear or a top or a boat, his face lit up with a smile. "And the joke will be even greater for those who only pretended to help." His smile grew broader.

Father Goswin had seen these smiles before and knew what they portended. "Now, Klaus," he warned. "You must not laugh. This is a holy edifice."

And so Klaus did not laugh, but it was a near thing. "They won't see me," he said. "The toys will appear on their doorsteps in the night, and in the morning the children will wake up and find them there—as if by Magic!"

Father Goswin crossed himself quickly. "As if by an angel, you mean," he said.

"If you like," Klaus said. "Now, the Eve of Christmas is coming in a few days. And I thought that would be a good night to make my deliveries." Klaus carefully placed his sack at the priest's feet. "So I've come to ask: Will you bless my toys?"

Father Goswin hesitated. He had blessed the sick. He had blessed women in childbirth. He had even blessed the occasional cow or goat. But toys? Playthings? This was new. And, perhaps, not entirely . . . appropriate?

Seeing the priest's hesitation, Klaus pressed his point. "Christmas is when we celebrate God's Son coming down and becoming a child, do we not? The shepherds gave the baby gifts, didn't they? And so did the astrologers."

"Wise men," the priest corrected him.

"So it's the perfect night to give my toys to the children: the night God gave us the gift of himself."

Well, when put that way . . . Father Goswin drew himself up and laid an ecclesiastical hand on the bulky sack. In his best pulpit voice he said, "Bless these toys, O Lord."

At that moment all the candles in the church blazed up suddenly brighter, a thing that had never happened before. The priest looked around, startled. For many weeks afterwards he pondered this singular occurrence. It was as if, he concluded finally, Heaven had approved his blessing. And he later preached a Christmas sermon that all toys, given and received in love, are holy. And he believed it. And in time, he also came to believe that the whole thing had been his idea.

On Christmas morning, as soon as there was light in the sky, Klaus stood outside his door and tried to be invisible while he watched and listened to what was happening all over the village below. He had gone out just after midnight on Christmas Eve, wrapped in a great, shapeless cloak, his bag slung over his back. He left the toys on doorsteps, believing that, as they had been blessed, no one would steal them. And no one did.

Now that it was the next morning, he listened with

great satisfaction to shouts of surprise and glee floating up to his cottage. A mother rose early to go out and feed the chickens—or a father opened the door just after frosty dawn to bring in some firewood—and they discovered the toys. Then they called for "Ilsa!" or "Gabriel!" or "Greta!" and the children came running because the voice sounded so glad. And the father or aunt or (in the grander houses) serving girl said, "Here is a marvelous doll for you. See, its arms and legs can move." Or, "Here is a carven deer. Look at its antlers!" Or, "Here is a boat. Someone must know how you love to play at the millpond." And then the children's eyes grew wide with wonder and delight, or their jaws dropped, or they whooped for joy—because it had been so long since they had had something of their own just for pure enjoyment and fun, and for some it was the very first time. And then the children hugged the dolls close or ran shouting down to the millpond with their boats or instantly named their bears and set them growling. Little Lena rattled her rattle, and the fifteen who received tops somehow found one another in the village market square and started a heated competition. And it was all more glorious and wonderful than anyone could ever have dreamed. Toys! Toys on Christmas Day!

All this Klaus saw and heard. And his heart told him

that he had found his vocation. Oh, he would still make chairs and cupboards. That was his job. But he knew from that hour what his real profession was. Because this joy that he felt did not just make him happy. It told him who he really was and would be all his days: a man who made toys and gave them away to children. And Klaus laughed his great laugh, and many in the village heard it boom out on this Christmas morning.

Klaus was convinced that not a soul in the village had even an inkling that it was he who had left the gifts on their doorsteps. In this he was quite wrong, and it shows how little he reckoned of his own reputation. Who else could do such ingenious carving? But, of course, when everyone saw how pleased he was to be walking amongst them anonymously, as he thought, they never breathed a word to him. And they were very severe with their children, warning them on pain of losing their toys not to reveal to Klaus what all knew.

Now, the next year was much like the first, except that the toys Klaus carved were even more ingenious. But the year after that things changed.

Klaus's village at the foot of Mount Feldberg was a market town, and that meant that people from surrounding hamlets and villages came there for fairs and feasts.

You know how things go. Children of Klaus's village played with children from other towns when they came in for the Saint Bartholomew's Day Fair. Those children were dazzled by the toys they saw; the children from Klaus's village made promises; and before he knew it, Klaus found himself responsible for making and delivering toys to two adjoining towns, each two miles away in opposite directions. So what had originally taken two months to make and an hour to deliver on Christmas Eve, now took four months of solid work and four nighttime hours of tramping around with an even bigger sack of toys. Klaus didn't mind. He loved his work. But he began to worry that he might not be able to complete all his deliveries on Christmas Eve—which was essential if his toys were to retain their Christmas blessing.

The year after, when Klaus turned twenty-four, he had five villages to visit and almost three hundred toys to make. He started the prodigious work of carving in early May so that he could be finished in time. He devised and tested an elaborate and demanding delivery plan that would only work if he started his rounds right after sundown. Accordingly, in December he posted—anonymously—strict instructions in the village market square. Parents must get children to bed very early on Christmas Eve. No toys would be delivered to a child peeping through a window or around a corner.

But on that Christmas Eve a ferocious storm blew up. Klaus had barely finished the delivery to the children in his own village before half the night was gone. He was cold and tired, and his cloak was soaked through. But he would not give up. There were children in those villages to the west and east and in the farmhouse on the Roman Road who were hoping, hoping for a toy. He would not let them down.

So he doggedly began the four-mile western trek. But before he had trudged much more than a mile through the knee-deep snow, he knew he was defeated. Strong as he was, he could not make the time he needed to get there and then out to the Roman Road before dawn—much less get to the eastern village. He flung himself and his enormous sack under a sheltering pine by the side of the road to wait out the storm. "It's no good," he sighed to the wind and the snow. "I've failed them."

It was as well that he did not know that at that very moment, Rolf Eckhof, whose jealousy and rage had only increased over the years, was stealing as many toys as he could from the doorways of Klaus's own beloved village. For that would have broken his heart. As it was, he almost wept from discouragement and frustration. He was going to let the children down and there was nothing he could do about it.

And that was the condition Klaus was in when a sleigh hung with two lanterns came racing toward him over the snow, pulled by a single, magnificent reindeer.

"Whoa, Dasher!" a voice called out, and the sleigh sliced to a halt, spraying snow everywhere like sparks from a fire. The reindeer snorted and stamped, as though it was impatient to run again. A figure swung gracefully off the sleigh's seat, grabbed one of the lanterns, and used it to peer at Klaus.

And the face the lantern revealed to him had the yellowest hair and the merriest, wildest blue eyes Klaus had ever seen. They both belonged to a rather striking young woman.

"You're just the man I need to see," the young woman said.

CHAPTER TWO

Anna the Racer

Klaus sprang to his feet in surprise, knocking his head on the lower branches of the pine tree under which he had been sheltering and covering himself with a shower of powdery snow. The young woman did not quite suppress a silvery giggle. Klaus didn't mind. In fact, even through an inch of snow, he found that he liked looking at her.

"You're just the man I need to see," she had said.

"I am?" Klaus now blurted out. "But how did you—"

"Let's talk on the sleigh," she interrupted. "Haven't you—something—to deliver?"

"Toys," he said as he brushed himself off.

"Toys?" said the young woman, and looked surprised. "Well, toys are not what I expected. But then, I didn't really know what to expect. Dasher! Will you pull this fine-looking young man and his sack of toys?" Fine-looking! Klaus liked that.

Dasher snorted and tossed his head as if to say, *I could pull twenty such and not strain a fetlock.*

Klaus lifted his sack into the sleigh, and they raced off into the snowstorm. And what with the truly alarming speed and the snow flying into their faces, and Klaus having to interrupt to shout directions every so often, it was hard to piece together the story the young woman told. But eventually he got it all, and it was this:

Her name was Anna. She was a stitcher and the daughter and granddaughter of stitchers. She could make any sort of garment, from the finest lace shawl to the toughest leather jerkin, and she loved all kinds of work with a needle. She was by nature spontaneous, so sometimes she worked into the most common coat or breeches sprays of spring flowers or likenesses of birds and beasts—and once a scene from the Battle of Jericho—embroidered in colorful threads. She loved to work in every color, but especially deep, true shades, and she had an absolute passion for red.

There was only one thing that Anna loved more than stitching, and that was racing in her sleigh. She did not compete against other drivers; they had given up contending against her long ago and banned her from their competitions. No, Anna raced the wind. And if she was spontaneous as a stitcher, she was hair-raisingly reckless as a driver. In this she was perfectly matched by her great-hearted reindeer, Dasher. Nothing made the two of them as happy as flying over open fields of fresh snow at breakneck speed—unless it was careening around the sharp corner of an icy road on one steel runner, the other flashing in the air.

That night Anna had had a dream, she said. "And it was the sort of dream you pay attention to. You know the kind I mean, Klaus," she shouted. They were on their way to the first village to deliver toys. Klaus noticed how nice his name sounded when Anna shouted it. So comforting and familiar, like she'd been shouting it all her life.

"I dreamed I was stitching a long coat and some breeches, both dyed a deep holly-berry crimson and made of supple deerskin." At this Dasher tossed his antlered head and snorted. "Oh, don't be silly, Dasher, it was just a dream," Anna called. "And then—now remember, this was a dream, you mustn't think I'm daft—"

"Oh, I won't," Klaus said, because he knew he never could.

"Well, in my dream, Dasher here put his head in my window while I was stitching and said—yes, you heard me: *said*—that's the daft part—'There's a man sitting under Three-Mile Pine, and you must go with me right now to get him. He has something urgent that must be delivered tonight.' And just as I was wondering how Dasher had grown clever enough to learn human speech, I woke up. And the dream was so vivid I knew I had to obey it. So that's why I was surprised when you told me that the urgent something was just some toys," she concluded.

"But they *are* urgent," Klaus said. And he told her all about the Black Death visiting his village and about its losses, and about the children helping and Father Goswin blessing the toys, and the growing list of children longing for one. "And so the toys are very urgent, Anna," Klaus concluded. "They bring happiness and fun and hope to the children. And they must all be delivered on Christmas Eve, because that is when they are blessed and will do the children the most good." And there was such concern and earnestness in Klaus's voice and demeanor that Anna impulsively squeezed his hand.

"Then deliver them all we shall!" she exclaimed. "Dasher, show this carpenter the meaning of speed!" And with a great bound Dasher ran away into the stormy night, and his speed was now so great that it was as if they had been standing still before and now they were flying. And what with the urgency he felt to deliver his toys and the increasing fascination he was feeling for Anna and the periodic surety he felt that he was about to be killed when the sleigh hit large bumps in the snow and actually did fly for a few feet, it was quite a night for Klaus.

They delivered toys safely to the doorstep of each house containing a child in every village, hamlet, and farm on Klaus's list. And they did it with ease. It was still four hours before the bell of the stone church in Klaus's village would toll Christmas matins when Anna delivered Klaus to his own doorstep. She put a hand briefly on his arm and jumped back into her sleigh before he could do anything but stammer his thanks. It had stopped storming, and the bright December moon had come out from behind the last of the clouds to cast its glow on the new snow. Klaus called after Anna, "Will I see you again?"

"That depends, carpenter," she called back.

"Depends on what?"

"Whether or not you like my proposal." Then she spoke to her reindeer. "On, Dasher!" she cried, and the sleigh shot away like an arrow.

Klaus's heart skipped a beat. "I'm—I'm sure I will!" he shouted after her. But he was not sure she had heard.

At daybreak Klaus returned to his doorstep after a few hours of sleep. Following his tradition of three years, he wanted to stand and listen to the exclamations of surprise and happiness when the children rushed out to see what he had brought them. He was particularly proud of a bird whistle he had devised that could sound very like a lark. He had made one for each child, and he wanted to hear the dawn chorus of the children blowing them—the sound of green spring in the midst of winter. He waited expectantly as the pale Christmas sun rimmed above the horizon. And a few moments later he heard what he had been listening for. First one lone bird from away over by the millpond, then another from the other side of the village, and then a whole chorus of larks. It was mixed with shouts of childish glee and wonder, and Klaus's heart swelled with satisfaction. It was all worth it, all the months of toil amongst the wood shavings and the supreme effort of the night before—all worth it just to hear those sweet sounds. He turned, smiling, to go back in for another hour or two of sleep when he heard another sound.

It was a wail. Klaus stood stock-still. It came from close by the market square. And then some child burst into tears right in the center of the village. And then, it seemed, howls of disappointment rose to meet his ears from all over town. It was a dismal din.

And that is when Klaus noticed amongst the smoke of half-a-hundred cook fires rising from village chimneys a thin stream of black coming from behind the Guild Hall. He raced over there as quickly as he could, without even putting on his coat. And what greeted him behind the Hall was a mound of smoldering ashes. Heedless of the heat, he reached into it and plucked out a charred wooden bear with movable legs—his signature toy.

It was all toys. Someone had made a fire of half the toys he had left on the doorsteps in his village. Not just someone, he suddenly knew with complete certainty: Rolf Eckhof.

Other men would have been angry. But Klaus did not understand anger. He only felt it once in his life—but that incident comes later in this chronicle. At this moment, he just stood helplessly holding his charred bear and wept.

And so it was that that Christmas half the children of

the little village below Mount Feldberg had no toy for a gift. And when they turned their tear-stained faces to their parents and asked why, I'm afraid more than one grown-up used the occasion for instruction. "Do you remember when you neglected to churn the butter and ran away to play instead?" a mother replied. "Hark back to the time in the summer when you pulled Gretchen's hair," a father sternly reminded. "You didn't mind." "You were sullen and surly." "You neglected your prayers." And the conclusion to all these faults was, "And so you got no toy this year. Klaus must have heard. Let it be a lesson for you, naughty child, and be better in the new year, and you may get a gift next Christmas." So alarmed was Klaus by this false and pernicious notion that he formally forsook his anonymity to try to correct it. "I just deliver toys," he said to all who would listen. "Who am I to discern hearts or mete out judgment?" But the myth that Klaus could know the moral condition of children and reward or punish them accordingly was so useful to parents that it persisted. And does to this day.

One day a few weeks into the new year, a thing happened for which Klaus had been waiting impatiently since the Eve of Christmas. It was the Frost Fair, when people from all the surrounding villages came to the market square to buy and sell winter goods. Klaus was there, selecting tools for his trade. He could not help but notice that some of the children looked very sad or gave him very black looks when he encountered them, and it burned his heart, but he comforted himself with the thoughts of the marvelous new toys he would make them for next Christmas. Only he did not at all know how he would prevent Rolf Eckhof's thefts, and this worried him.

Then in a shower of sprayed snow, and a cry of "Watch out!" from someone, Anna was suddenly there. She strode right over to him.

"Where can I get beeswax for my runners?" she demanded of him, as though they were resuming a conversation instead of seeing each other for the first time in weeks. And then: "It's my first Frost Fair, you know."

All that day Klaus and Anna spent together, going from booth to booth and pretending to be interested in the wares. And those who loved Klaus were glad to see the young man with the flaming hair and beard—it was a rich, full beard now—made so happy, even if it was by a foreigner from outside the village.

In the evening, Klaus took Anna up to his cottage, and they had a supper of bread with honey and cured meats and winter apples. The latter, with some stored grain, made an excellent meal for Dasher, who waited outside polishing his antlers against the trunk of a bare linden tree. Anna deplored and poured scorn on Klaus's scanty wardrobe of a few ragged and rusty-colored smocks and breeches and coats. But she marveled at the many beautiful and useful things he had made for his home: sliding pocket doors and carved shelves and a table with removable leaves. It all put Anna in mind of the parting statement she had made to Klaus on Christmas morning.

"About my proposal," she said. Klaus swallowed hard. He had been waiting all day for her to introduce this subject and had hardly been able to keep himself from bringing it up.

"I accept," he blurted out.

"But you haven't heard it yet," she scoffed.

"Oh. Yes. Go on," Klaus said.

"Dasher needs a house. I would like you to build him one."

It was, if not the very last thing Klaus had expected her to say, then very, very close to it. "A house," he said. "For your reindeer."

"And it must be a good one," Anna went on. She looked around. "Twice as big as this one. With all your lovely counters and shelves and a great carven bed. Twice as big as yours."

"But he's a reindeer," Klaus exclaimed. Anna frowned. "A very remarkable reindeer, to be sure," Klaus hastily added. "But still . . . you know . . ." he finished weakly.

"Yes?" she said.

"Well. A bed? Shelves? I suppose he'll want an icebox and a cookstove and a privy out back?"

"Naturally," she said.

"But, Anna, why?" Klaus burst out.

She smiled. "Oh, you needn't know that. You just build the house."

"I see," he said.

"And in exchange, I will give you a sleigh. A very fine, fast sleigh with room enough in it for all your toys, even if you end up delivering to every house in the Black Forest. And," she added with a slight frown that Klaus did not recall or understand until much, much later, "Dasher and I will help you with your deliveries next Christmas Eve. If you like."

"I do! I would!" Klaus said instantly. "But what about the Christmas Eve after that?" He was trying to be sly and drive a hard bargain.

"We'll see," Anna replied.

Klaus looked into Anna's sky blue eyes. For one whole half-second he considered how truly mad her proposal was. "I accept," he said.

"Good," she said. And they shook on it. "And you will build Dasher's house right here beside your own."

"You don't wish me to build it in your own village?" he asked, surprised.

"I'm certain this is where Dasher wants his house," she replied. "He likes the view."

So it was that all through the frosty winter, in addition to making his livelihood, Klaus built Dasher a house next to his own. When it came time to set the crucks in place, the young men of the village came to help, and then they all toasted the frame with winter ale and spoke of their marriage prospects. And though Klaus kept silent, carrying, as he believed, his desire to wed Anna as a secret in his heart, the others grinned because, in truth, the thought was written all over his face.

And when spring came at last and with it the chattering of the millstream again into the pond, the children collected reeds there and dried them in the sun for Klaus, as they had done after the plague, and the Master Thatcher helped him make his roof. Then there was more toasting

when the roof was in place, this time with new spring wine.
And so the outside of Dasher's house was finished.

But this was only the beginning for Klaus. Because now
the inside needed doing. The furnishings, all the carving
and carpentry, he felt, must be done by himself, alone.
Only the finest, he said to himself, for Dasher. So, through
the spring and the summer, he set himself to making and
carving the new, bigger bed, the shelves and chests of
drawers, the table and chairs. And, most absurd of all—
and Klaus couldn't help but chuckle as he built it—the
privy out back that Dasher would be unable even to enter,
let alone want to use.

And because he was now also making this year's toys as
well as all the new house furnishings, and working for his
own livelihood on top of that, he was busier than at any
other time in his twenty-five years of living. Yet he was
happy, as he always was once he knew what there was to do
and was doing it. So when a delegation from a village away
on the other side of Mount Feldberg, where Klaus had
never been, came to tell him that his fame had reached
them and to ask him if their children might possibly be
squeezed into this year's Christmas Eve deliveries, a smile
wreathed his face, he said yes without hesitation, and

asked for directions. But when the delegation left, very happy with the news they would be taking back to the other side of Mount Feldberg, Klaus thought, *This sleigh Anna is giving me had better be very fast indeed.*

Anna visited often. Claiming a thorough acquaintance with Dasher's tastes and preferences, she frequently directed the shape or carving or color of a particular item. When she paid unusually close attention to the cookstove, which Klaus intended to buy at the Fall Fair, it was his turn to laugh. "Why should Dasher be so particular about the size of the firebox?" he asked. "He has hoofs! He won't even be able to open the door!"

Anna took great offense at this. "Do not presume, Klaus, just because your hair is so red and fine, to know the ways of reindeer. The firebox must be just as I have said."

And so Klaus shook his head of fine red hair and did as she wished. In truth it was a pleasure to him to do as Anna wished.

And when once again the snow began to fly in the village under the mountain, and the ice began to creep, day by day, from the edges to the middle of the millpond, the house was completed. And so was Klaus's new batch of toys. This year he was featuring Noah's Arks with animals two by two and was quite happy with the way the lions had turned out, having copied them from the bestiary Father Goswin kept in the stone church. And, of course, there were lots of bears and tops and whistles, too.

"When will Dasher move in?" Klaus asked Anna. The reindeer's house was now well and truly finished, inside and out.

"When there is enough snow on the ground for him to pull your new sleigh to you," Anna replied.

So now Klaus sat in his own house and waited impatiently for the first real storm of the autumn.

At last it came, blowing in fast from the north in the night and depositing enough sugary new snow to fill all the lanes and drift up to the top step of Klaus's cottage. Then, shortly before dawn, the storm blew itself south, and when the sun came up, it shone on a hushed, white world.

And on that sunny winter day Anna came, driving Klaus's new sleigh.

Behind it was hitched her own, and both were filled with bags and parcels and bolts of cloth and clutches of ribbons and woolen threads all the colors of the rainbow. And sticking out behind Anna's sleigh was a tall-case clock. Dasher made nothing of the extra weight. He trotted briskly, his antlers trimmed with red ribbons, in high spirits to be coming to his new house. Anna drove through the lanes of the village, and the villagers, sensing by common knowledge that something special was about to happen, followed behind her.

So that by the time Anna glided to a stop in front of the two houses—Klaus's and the new one—the whole village was following in a train behind. They crowded around as Anna leapt lightly to the ground.

"What do you think of your new sleigh, Klaus?" she asked.

"Splendid," he replied. And it was. It was trimmed in red and gold and far larger and more regal than he needed, he thought, but so sleek and swift-looking that on any other occasion he would have longed to jump in it then and there and let Dasher take him for a ride.

But this was not any other occasion. "How do you like Dasher's new house?" he asked Anna. And all the crowd listened anxiously, breathless to know her answer.

Anna turned to her reindeer. "What do you say, Dasher?" she asked. "Is it suitable?" The reindeer bugled his approval loudly and stamped the snowy ground. The village cheered.

But Anna smiled. "A house? For a reindeer?" she asked. "What can you be thinking, Klaus?"

Klaus smiled back. "Yes, when you come to think of it, it *is* a silly idea."

"Can you think of a better one? Or is your head only good for growing splendid red hair?"

And suddenly Klaus *could* think of a better idea. Or rather, having been thinking of it for almost a whole year, it finally rushed up from his heart to his mouth. He got down on a knee in the snow. "Anna," he asked, "will you come and live with me in Dasher's house?"

"As your wife, I hope you mean," she said.

Klaus blushed scarlet. "Yes, yes, of course," he said quickly.

"Yes, yes, of course," she replied just as quickly. "Dasher can live in your old house."

Such a loud and sustained cheer went up from the villagers that it could almost be heard on the other side of Mount Feldberg. And without further ado, the crowd unloaded Anna's belongings from the sleighs and bustled them into the new house, taking care not to damage her tall-case clock. And then they placed Anna and Klaus on two of Klaus's new chairs and carried them down to the stone church, where Father Goswin joined them together as husband and wife, delivering also an edifying sermon on the joys and rigors of the married state.

Finally, when everyone had gone outside and a great bonfire had been lit in the market square for warmth and jollity, Anna produced a large package. "It's your wedding gift, Klaus. Open it." Inside was the most splendid thing Klaus had ever seen. Indeed, it was so splendid that everyone, just on the edge of starting a very boisterous wedding celebration, stopped what they were doing and grew hushed when Klaus drew it from its wrappings and held it up.

It was a long coat, with breeches and a hat, all made from the finest, softest, thickest wool. They were dyed the deepest holly-berry crimson and trimmed in white ermine. Two leaping reindeer were embroidered on the front of the coat, one on either side of the buttons. They were, in truth, garments for a king, not a village carpenter.

"I will not have my husband cold on Christmas Eve!" Anna declared, and gave Klaus a resounding kiss.

At that the loudest cheer of the day went up, and the wedding party roared to a start.

But lurking at the edge of the crowd, because he could not stay away from the happiest day in Klaus's life, was unhappy Rolf Eckhof. And seeing Klaus's joy and all the vil-

lage joining in it, jealousy and rage rose in him like a rav-
enous hunger. For a moment Klaus's eye happened to catch
his, and Klaus saw in it all Rolf Eckhof's malice and hatred
for him.

And in the midst of all his bliss, he felt a stab of dread.
For Klaus knew that now his trouble was just beginning.

CHAPTER THREE

The Magic Reindeer

The wedding of Klaus and Anna was so glorious and merry and filled-to-bursting with good food and drink that everyone in the village under Mount Feldberg talked about it for three months. It was simply the most memorable matrimony anyone could recall.

Klaus and Anna, meanwhile, settled quickly and contentedly into married life—just as though the two of them had been made for marriage and for each other, which of course they had. Dasher would not set hoof into Klaus's house but only fixed Anna and Klaus with a defiant stare when they tried to usher him across the threshold. So Klaus built Dasher a fine and sturdy stable on the other side of the new house instead, which was much more practical, and gave his old house to the Worshipful Guild of Foresters, Carpenters, and Woodworkers as a residence for retired widowers. So it was a satisfactory arrangement all around.

Now it will be recalled that Klaus and Anna's nuptials fell just a few weeks before Christmas Eve and also that Klaus had agreed to include in this year's delivery of Christmas toys a village on the far side of Mount Feldberg.

And so it fell that on one clear, cold evening in mid-December, Anna and Klaus were lying snug in their large carved bed doing what they so often did in those early newlywed days. That is, Anna was embroidering a scene of the bloody and drunken battle of the Centaurs and Lapiths onto a coverlet she had just stitched, and Klaus was polishing off the last of her rabbit stew with sugared almonds— for Anna had found that with her new stove she liked cooking very much, and Klaus had found that he liked it, too.

But this night Anna could not help but notice that Klaus ate his last bit of bread and sucked every drop of gravy from his fingers in a distracted, worried manner. "Are you concerned about delivering to the new village, Klaus?" Anna asked.

"Not at all," he said. "With Dasher, we'll make short work of the trip." He sighed.

"Is it the toys? Are there not enough?"

"More than enough." Another sigh, somewhat deeper.

"You're unhappy with their design this year. Not sufficiently ingenious."

"The cleverest I've ever made," Klaus replied miserably, and sighed deeper still.

"Then what is wrong, husband? All this sighing is doleful music."

"Nothing," Klaus said, and sighed so profoundly that in his stable Dasher looked up from his evening mash.

Anna put down her needle. She had just come to the part in the battle where a Centaur was smashing a well-aimed hoof into the eye of a Lapith, all purple and red and black threads, and it was hard to leave off there, but she did. She looked at Klaus. "Husband," she said, "you are the least skilled liar in the known world. Now tell me what is wrong."

And then with a cry of distress Klaus threw back the covers, scattering Anna's stitching to the four posters, and paced the floor. He told her everything: how last Christmas half the toys he had delivered had been stolen from the village doorsteps and burned in a fire behind the Guild Hall, how it had wrung his heart to see the disappointed looks on children's faces, and how the doer of the evil deed had given him a stare of such naked malevolence at their wedding that he knew he would try to repeat his misdeed this Christmas Eve. He stopped his pacing and looked at Anna in anguish. "And how am I to prevent it?" he concluded. "How can I stop Rolf Eckhof? I cannot think of a way!"

Nor could Anna, at first.

But then her eye lighted on the scattered skeins of thread, and she clapped her clever hands together because suddenly she knew the answer. "You have married me in the very nick of time," she announced.

And so it was that on that year's Christmas Eve, clad in his splendid new red coat and breeches, Klaus found himself shuffling cautiously along the roof of the first house on his delivery rounds. He looked down at Anna standing in the sleigh.

"You're doing very well," Anna hissed up to him encouragingly.

Klaus found that he did not have quite the head for heights he had imagined, but in another few steps he was at the chimney (and luckily in those days chimneys were very short). He peered down it and saw only darkness. Good. No fire burning down below. Then he let down the toy he was carrying—one of his signature bears—by one of Anna's embroidery threads. When it was a few inches above the fireplace, he swung the thread wide and let it go—and heard the bear land satisfyingly on the floor beyond the hearth. *Thump!* He had just delivered, for the very first time, a Christmas toy down a chimney—and thus safe from the thievery of Rolf Eckhof. He turned around and grinned at Anna down below. "Thank you for thinking of this," he mouthed. She helped him down from the roof and they were quickly off to the next house.

True, letting toys down chimneys—or simple smoke holes, as many of the village houses had instead—took extra time. And true also, Klaus landed a few toys in smoldering remnants of nighttime fires at first and had to try again with a second toy. But the novel deliveries only had to be made in his own village, where Rolf Eckhof was lurking. And with Dasher's speed he and Anna easily made up the time on the rest of their appointed rounds, including the village on the other side of the mountain. They were home three hours before the matins bell chimed in the icy Christmas dawn. And amid the clamor and glee of the children, which floated up to their house as they stood tired but satisfied, arm in arm, on their doorstep, they did not hear one wail or sob. All the blessed toys were safe.

Nor did they hear the muffled shrieks of rage and frustration from inside Rolf Eckhof's house. He had indeed been out on Christmas Eve but had found no toys to steal. Now he tried to shut out all the happiness assaulting his ears by covering them with his two feather pillows, but found that he could not. His mind was poisoned now, almost beyond reason or reclaiming, and any success of Klaus's or crossing of his own plans heated his blood so intolerably that to cool it he had to smash or rend whatever object his eye lit upon. This he did now, and I'm afraid his house suffered for it—starting with the feather pillows, which he tore so violently that for a whole minute there was a blizzard inside his house. But an hour afterwards he sat on the floor, for he had broken all his chairs, and brooded his revenge in cold, clear anger. He did not know what he would do. He did not know when he would think of it. But he knew that he would. And Rolf Eckhof was the sort of man who could wait.

And so the years flew by, and no man can stop their flight; nor should they try. Each Christmas Eve, Klaus and Anna and Dasher delivered toys to a wider and wider realm of children. Each year, just before they set out, a tiny frown flickered across Anna's face—unnoticed by Klaus—and something she longed to say came all the way to her lips, but then got no further when Klaus took her hand and with great delight escorted her into the sleigh. And each year, Klaus became more and more expert at letting toys down chimneys and smoke holes as a ward against Rolf Eckhof, until it became his preferred method of toy delivery—though in truth Rolf Eckhof never again tried to steal Christmas toys. People in all the villages learned to damp down their fires before they retired on Christmas Eve. It wasn't long before Klaus devised a special knot that he could undo with a deft flick of his wrist just as a toy came to rest on a floor, leaving it standing upright and allowing him to whisk its thread back up the chimney. And in this way the legend grew that somehow Klaus was taking the toys down the chimney himself, an absurd notion which persists to this day despite Klaus having scattered physics textbooks amongst his Christmas deliveries in recent years.

For a jest some tucked the toys Klaus delivered into the freshly washed stockings they set on their hearths to dry, or placed them under the evergreen boughs they hung about their houses as a reminder that though the world was frozen, spring would come again.

Anna and Klaus continued in their professions, for their need of extra means to purchase wood and carving tools grew greater and greater. Anna stitched. Klaus joined and worked wood. Each year was busier than the year before. Still, Anna found time to indulge her new passion for cooking ever more sumptuous meals, and Klaus found time to eat them. And since Anna's dishes tended more—much more—toward the gravy and dumpling and goose variety— still and always Klaus's favorite meal—than they did toward the celery and cottage cheese and one-single-radish-on-a-plate variety, Klaus's girth improved wonderfully. And when, after years of selfless toil, Anna hit on the miraculous maple sugar cookie recipe for which she became so justly renowned, Klaus was finally able to fulfill the prophecy with which the villagers had teased him during that first year after the Black Death: "You'll grow fat if you keep eating like that!"

"So be it," he had said then, and "So be it," he said now, as he kissed his talented wife. "So long as Dasher doesn't mind the extra weight and the villagers' roofs hold, so be it!"

But Anna's culinary talents did not extend only to Klaus. No person in the village under Mount Feldberg ever went hungry if Anna could help it. So long as her larder held out, Anna fed all and sundry, and Heaven help anyone who tried to resist a second helping of anything. They got a tongue-lashing about keeping up their strength and were then watched over until they had eaten everything she had made for them. And so, when the harvests were good, all girths improved as the years rolled by.

But specially did Anna see to the retired widowers of the Worshipful Guild of Foresters, Carpenters, and Woodworkers. They had made of Klaus's old house an ever-expanding warren as each took up his tools and added on his own room. But they took their meals in a splendid common dining hall they had labored together to construct. The joke went round the Guild that you had better retire hungry because Anna was going to fill you right up to the brim once she got you in that hall. In due course, Father Goswin, having heard the joke, moved in, even though he was not a member of the Guild and had not retired. "You all need spiritual guidance in your waning years," he said. "Pass me the shepherd's pie." He was welcomed, and he soon wrote a moving epistle to the Bishop about how he

had founded this charitable institution for widowers—
which was no more than he came to believe.

If the years were busy for Klaus and Anna, they were
also jolly. Both knew the deep contentment of loving the
useful work they did. They scarcely noticed the advancing
streaks of white in their hair—and Klaus's beard—and
they certainly paid no attention to the lines that laughter
brought to their faces. In their hearts and in the hardihood
of their bodies, they seemed age-proof. If they had one sorrow, it was that no children of their own had come to
them. But then, as Klaus often said, and Anna agreed, it
tempts fate ("Heaven," Father Goswin corrected them)
for two happy people to have all they desire, and surely they
felt a stake in the lives of hundreds of children throughout
the villages of the Black Forest.

Life went on like this pleasantly for years and years and
still more years.

And then something extraordinary happened.

One summer Rolf Eckhof turned up at the retirement
home. Certainly he had reached retirement age, and he
was not a widower only because he had never married.
Some thirty-one years had passed since his mischief with
the toys—which Klaus had never revealed to anyone but

Anna—and no sequel had followed. But no one expected to see him standing at the door with his possessions in a cart behind him.

"I have a right to be here," he barked at the Guild member who answered the door. "I have worked hard all my life."

Well, how could he be refused? As Father Goswin noted, even the uncharitable have a claim on charity. He had made his life a lonely, bitter one, but still his loneliness was real. "Rolf Eckhof may share my room," said one of the kinder widowers, "until he builds his own."

Which Rolf Eckhof soon did. And if it was not as skillfully made as some others in the winding old house, no one was tactless enough to comment on it. And certainly Rolf Eckhof seemed to be a new man in retirement. He did not actually smile, nor did he ever do much talking, but he did help. Having cooked and cleaned for himself all his life— which few in the house had done—he made himself useful all around the place, but specially around the cookstove. And anyone who cooks will always find some welcome wherever he goes.

Soon even Klaus and Anna reconciled with their old enemy. And though their doing so has been much criticized in the court of historical opinion, I have always maintained that, despite what happened later, they did right to forgive him.

On the Christmas Eve after Rolf Eckhof came to the retirement house, Klaus readied himself for a long night of deliveries. The very last village in the Black Forest had been added to his rounds at the Saint Bartholomew's Fair that summer, and so he would be traveling farther than ever. In his enormous toy bag—now a dozen flour sacks stitched together and embroidered all over by Anna with likenesses of Roman emperors and mythical beasts and constellations major and minor—were over six hundred toys. This year's new item was a puzzle box made of white pine and ash that opened if one pushed and pulled sliding panels in just the right way. Inside each was a flower seed, so that the children could look forward through the winter to planting it in the spring and seeing what kind of vegetable or flower it would be.

Klaus heaved the huge sack into the sleigh. Dasher stamped the snow, eager to be off, as impatient as ever. For though the weight he pulled had grown steadily over the years due to the increase in the number of toys and the belt size of their maker, it was still a trifle to him. Klaus hesitated. A corner of his heart was heavy. Anna was not coming with him, and it was the first time this had happened.

"I'm just feeling under the weather, Klaus. It's nothing to worry about," she had said.

"I won't go. It's just one year."

"Not go! What utter nonsense. You are responsible for our children. If you don't bring them toys, their parents will make up any number of reasons why they don't deserve them."

"But, Anna, if you're ill and need looking after—"

She had fixed him with her bright blue eyes. "Do not presume, carpenter, that because you are the handsomest man in the Black Forest, you know anything about leechcraft. I will be fine. I have made a broth. Master Eckhof has brought me the herbs." Then she had laughed her silvery laugh that dispelled all gloom, and he had felt much better.

Except for that one small corner of his heart. And as the night wore on, the troubled feeling in that corner spread and spread.

Klaus and Dasher delivered the toys to the houses of his own village in good time as well as to the three villages east and west, but for the first time it brought Klaus no real pleasure. He was distracted. *Is Anna all right?* he kept wondering. *Should I have left her?* Dasher was racing up the steep track that went over a shoulder of Mount Feldberg and was just clearing the tree line when Klaus suddenly signaled for him to stop. The sleigh slid to a halt. Dasher snorted once, and then all was silent. The winter stars and half a moon glimmered down on the two. Klaus got out of the sleigh and stood beside it.

He did not know why he had stopped. He had never done so before unless there was a runner that wanted fixing or a harness buckle to adjust. But now he felt a need to be still. Something was happening, he felt, though he did not know what.

He looked down into the valley at his village. Waves of frigid air rose up from there and made him shiver. He pulled his crimson coat close, but he could not get warm. The cold current made him feel exhausted to his very bones. He caught a glimpse of his beard, almost all white now, as it caught the icy breeze and danced before his eyes. *I'm old,* he thought, *too old to keep making these deliveries.* For it seemed to Klaus that the weight of the years he had ignored for so long now piled themselves upon him all at once. They made him stoop and stagger.

At this Dasher grew alarmed. He stamped a hoof and snorted again. He rubbed Klaus with his glossy flank, as if trying to rally him. He caught Klaus's gaze in his large, brown reindeer's eyes, and to Klaus it seemed as if those eyes were urging him to do something. But what? He was so tired. Impulsively he threw his arms around Dasher's neck, his own eyes filling with sad and weary tears.

"Great heart," he spoke low into the ear of the beast, "I feel my strength is gone. I feel I'm at the end of things. What shall I do?"

Now it happened that Dasher had been waiting through all these decades for Klaus to speak to him spirit to spirit. For though he was Anna's deer, in truth he had been made for Klaus. And now that Klaus had finally spoken to him not as a man talks idly to a beast but as one soul seeks out another, Dasher was able at last to reply.

"Your strength is not gone, Klaus," he said. "Indeed, the beginning of your true strength is about to come upon you."

"Are you—are you *speaking* to me, old friend?" Klaus asked Dasher in amazement.

"I am," Dasher said. "You have spoken to me as one soul to another. And that has unleashed the Magic. Cover your ears, O Man!" And then Dasher threw back his great antlered head and bugled as no reindeer had ever bugled before or ever has since. The sky rang with the immense sound as it echoed and re-echoed up into the Heavens. Then silence fell while Jupiter, Klaus's Jovial star, beamed benevolently down on them.

"What will happen now?" Klaus asked in an awed whisper.

"Wait and see," Dasher said. In the hush, the mountain, the man, and the reindeer, the very air, seemed poised for something—something even more extraordinary than Dasher finding speech at last. Klaus caught a scent in the air, clean and bracing. *Why, it's peppermint*, he realized, and felt much better. Still he waited.

Then he heard the joyful sound of sleigh bells. He looked back down the track to see who was approaching. But the sound wasn't coming from the track. Nor was it coming from anywhere on the shoulder of the mountain or from the valley below.

It was coming from above Klaus's head.

He looked up in wonder, and this is what he saw: Coming fast from the north, cleaving the cold air in strict formation, were seven reindeer, six almost as large and deep-chested as Dasher; the seventh, a female, more dainty. And these reindeer were flying—not metaphorically, but really, truly flying. Swift as eagles, fast as racehorses, they galloped through a bank of cloud, and their antlers flashed in the moonlight as they scattered it in all directions. "I have seen many astonishing sights in my life," Klaus reported years later, "but none to compare with that. They were so fierce and alive, coming on like quicksilver, flashing across the sky. I shall never forget it." And nor does anyone else who has had the privilege of seeing that sight.

One of the reindeer gripped a harness in its teeth, and it was the bells from this that Klaus was hearing. All alighted and pressed up against Dasher, as though to reacquaint themselves with him. "It has been long, brother," Klaus heard one say. Dasher looked at Klaus and saw his deep bewilderment.

"We are not demons, Klaus, nor angels. We are reindeer, just as you see us. But we were awakened long ago for this very purpose. For the moment when your burden would prove too taxing. Harness us."

And so, in a kind of dream, Klaus unhitched Dasher's tack from the front of the sleigh and replaced it with the new harness. With Dasher in the lead, all eight reindeer stepped into their traces as one, and Klaus buckled them in. "Now get in the sleigh, Klaus, and hang on. For we," Dasher shouted as all the reindeer pawed the snow, "are the Eight Flyers!" And just as Klaus found his seat in the sleigh—and not a split second too soon—the reindeer leapt into the air like arrows shot from a bow.

Klaus's first flight was more glorious than any of us who have not ridden in a sleigh pulled by flying reindeer can ever know. After a few moments of initial vertigo and not knowing up from down, he took to flying in his sleigh as if he had been born to it, which of course he had. He exulted in the wind blowing through his hair and at the sight of the sleeping villages below and the wheeling stars above. And when he thought of how quickly he would be able to get his toys to the children now, and then when he thought that he could be let down to a roof rather than having to climb up to it, and then finally when he thought how quickly he would be back by Anna's side, sheer joy bubbled up in him. "Hee, hee, hee!" he began. And then, "Ha, ha, ha!" he noted as he warmed to his theme. And then, finally, in his deep, rich bass, "Ho, ho, ho!" he laughed as he sailed through the roaring winter night.

Klaus was through with his deliveries so early on this astonishing Christmas Eve that he thought for once he would be able to get half a good night's sleep. The Flyers landed the sleigh with a hiss of runners between his house and Dasher's stable. "Thank you, Comet. Thank you, Vixen, my girl," he said. "Thank you, Cupid and Donner and Prancer and Blitzen and Dancer." He put a hand on Dasher's neck. "And thank you, my old friend. What a night!"

"Good night, Klaus," said Dasher. He yawned like a

cavern. "We'll sleep under the pines tonight. Sort accommodations out in the morning." And he trotted away with his brothers and sister.

Through the window Klaus saw a candle lit in their bedroom. He smiled to think how surprised Anna would be to see him home so early.

But when he got to his bedroom, what he saw at first was not Anna, but Father Goswin. He was sitting in a chair drawn up to their big bed, dressed in his church vestments and murmuring Latin. When Klaus entered the room, the priest looked up, and Klaus saw the tears on his face. Then he saw his beloved wife, small and still under the coverlet on the bed, her eyes closed. He did not understand. Anna was never still.

"I'm so sorry," Father Goswin said. "I have administered the Last Rites."

Klaus collapsed in a swoon.

Rolf Eckhof, of course, had fled long ago.

CHAPTER FOUR

The Green Council Convenes

Klaus was dreaming. In his dream he was racing in a sleigh drawn by eight reindeer up a tremendously steep, shining Road of ice that ran straight and true, right into the sky. It was dawn, and as the sun rose, Klaus glimpsed above the gilded clouds a far, wintry country. There were parklands and mountains and a waterfall spilling through a hole in a frozen lake. In the midst of it all was a magnificent castle of green and silver and pearl. *I'm going home,* Klaus thought in his dream. *Home to Anna.*

But the thought of Anna brought Klaus's dream to a dark, abrupt end, as though all the light had suddenly been snatched from the world. He struggled to wake up. Sleep still clouded his memory, but he knew something terrible beyond calculation had happened, something to his beloved wife. And then suddenly, with a sickening shock, he remembered.

"Anna!" he called out in anguish before he even opened his eyes.

A familiar hand took his. A familiar voice said, "Yes, dear Klaus. I'm here. Merry Christmas!"

Klaus opened his eyes, and there she was. Anna, as real and warm and alive as ever. He sat bolt upright in bed, for that was where he was, and hugged her tight. Then he held her at arm's length and looked at her in wonder. "Aren't you dead, Anna?" he asked.

"Not anymore," she said. "It's best I not be, apparently." Klaus looked as confused at this as you or I would have been. "Oh, I was dead. Killed by Rolf Eckhof's herbs, which I was fool enough to put into my broth."

"Last night, out on the mountain, I felt something," Klaus said. "Something cold coming up from down here in the valley."

"I think that must have been the hate and spite of poor Rolf Eckhof."

"*Poor* Rolf Eckhof!" Klaus growled. "When I find him, I'll stuff his herbs down his throat!"

"That's how I felt, too, at first," said Anna thoughtfully. "I wanted to tear him limb from limb after I died. Or at least haunt him. But then they talked to me, and, well, I don't feel that way now."

Klaus paid no attention. He sprang from the bed. "Where is he?" he roared, and glared around the bedroom as though Rolf Eckhof might be hiding behind a chest of drawers. (And it was lucky for Rolf Eckhof that he was not.) His hard carpenter's hands were in fists and his gentle face was twisted with rage. "Where is Eckhof!?"

"Calm down, Klaus," Anna said mildly.

"I *am* calm!" Klaus yelled. "Where are my boots?"

"No, Klaus," said Anna, and took one of his fists and kissed it. "We don't have to worry about any of that. Isn't it lucky?"

"But he harmed you!" Klaus growled, though, to his annoyance, he found that Anna's kiss had dissipated a good deal of his anger.

"He killed me dead," she replied cheerfully and kissed

his other fist. And then she smiled dazzlingly at him. It was no good. The last vestige of the only real anger Klaus had ever felt in his life promptly deserted him. He took his wife in his arms. "Oh, Anna!" he said. "I'm so glad you're here!" And he gave her a resounding kiss.

"Yes," she said. "They decided that was better than taking you over. So I'm alive again now, good as new."

"They?" Klaus asked.

"The ones who brought me back. The ones who laid you on our bed after you swooned. Which was very sweet of you to do."

"But who are they?" Klaus asked.

"It's time you met them." She steered him to the bedroom door, opened it, and led him through.

Klaus was never sure later how to describe what greeted his eyes next. The rest of his and Anna's house was mostly one all-purpose living room where they cooked and worked and drew chairs up to the fireplace. But at first he could find no trace of that room. Where was the cookstove? Where were the table and chairs, where the familiar hearth? Ah, there they were. He could just make them out scattered around the edges of a new room that had displaced and was at least three times larger than the old one.

"So for that Christmas Day," Klaus reported later, "our house was bigger inside than it was outside."

Right in the center of this new room was a beautiful round table surrounded by six chairs so tall and carven that they looked like thrones—Klaus could not help but admire the workmanship. Four of the chairs were occupied.

"We sent the priest home," said one of the people sitting at the table. He was a tall man with a long sweeping beard and a kindly expression, and like the other three sitting with him, he glowed faintly. "He will not remember that we were here. He will recall only that he did something quite stupendously heroic to save Anna's life." He grinned affectionately at the thought of Father Goswin. "No doubt he will make a sermon of it, taking full credit. Sit down, Klaus, sit down. Yes, these thrones are meant for you and Anna!"

So Klaus and Anna sat shyly at the table and looked around at the others. Never had they been in such company!

"I am your namesake, Klaus," said the man with the kindly face. "In my own country a thousand years ago I was called Nikolaos. Or as you would say, Nicholas."

"*Saint* Nicholas," said one of the other men at the table,

raising his finger. He was the color of burnished black walnut wood.

"A thousand years ago!" Klaus blurted out. "But how can that be?"

"Because he is dead, of course," the burnished man said impatiently. "Or what you would call dead. We all are."

"This is Saint Babukar," Nicholas said. "He was one of the wise astrologers who sought and found the Holy Infant."

Babukar stood and bowed to Klaus. "Here they call me Balthazar. They have never been to Africa, so I do not blame them."

I have stumbled into a world of wonders, thought Klaus. *A day ago I would not have believed a reindeer could talk. Or fly. And now I am in the company of Saints.*

"I am Abigail," said a quiet woman sitting on the other side of Nicholas.

"You will have heard of her," Babukar said. "For she it was that when that son of a jackal—"

"Babukar!" cried Nicholas.

"Sorry." Babukar rose and bowed again. "I meant to say, when that *innkeeper* would not give a room to the Holy Family, she it was who led them to the stable." Anna looked at Abigail, and the Saint turned and held her gaze for a moment. She radiated a compassion and empathy so intense that Anna felt a strong desire to tell her about the one sorrow lodged in her heart. *But no*, thought Anna, *that is not why they have come.*

"And this is Saint Farouk," Nicholas said of a handsome man with jet-black hair and a neatly clipped beard. "He was a herder of sheep, the first to leave his flock and hasten to the stable when he heard the glad tidings." Farouk rose, touched his fingers to his forehead and his breast, and then bowed with an elegant flourish. "The blessings of all Animal Creation be upon you," he said.

"Now, Klaus," Nicholas said, "like you, I know something about slipping gifts into houses late at night. And so I am head of this commission. We are called the Green Council, named for all that stays alive in the winter."

"And we others," said Abigail, "were drawn into the Council because of our devotion to the Child whose winter feast you honor with your toy deliveries."

"You know about those?" Klaus asked in some surprise.

"All Heaven knows of them," said Abigail.

"That is why we are here," Nicholas said. "You see, last night you unleashed the Magic of Christmas."

"I didn't mean to!" Klaus said hastily. "It was an accident!"

"No, no, Klaus, you did well," Nicholas said with a re-assuring chuckle.

"I watch the sky always," said Babukar excitedly. "And I can tell you that the stars were aligned perfectly for the event! Did you not see them, Klaus? Especially your birth star of Jupiter!"

"Dasher had waited so long for you to speak to him!" said Farouk. "Animals always know far more than we think. When you spoke to Dasher and he replied, we could no longer be kept away."

"And that proved well for your wife," concluded Nicholas.

Klaus reached over and squeezed Anna's hand. "I thank you a thousand times," he said, "for bringing her back to me."

"This Eckhof is the son of a desert hyena!" Babukar banged the table with his fist.

"Why must you always insult the Animal Creation?" asked Farouk indignantly.

Babukar rose and bowed again. "I meant no offense."

Nicholas turned to Klaus. "It is your work that we have come about," he said. "We are here to help you. That is," and he and the other three Saints around the table turned intently toward Klaus, "if you choose to continue it."

"What do you mean?" asked Klaus, a little uneasy at having four Saints scrutinize him.

"Well, you have a choice, of course," Nicholas said. "If you did not, what you do would have no value."

"Oh," said Klaus. "I see." He reflected for a moment or two. Silence reigned at the table.

"Klaus?" Saint Nicholas asked gently. "Do you choose to continue making your Christmas Eve deliveries?"

Well. Klaus thought of how weary he had been last night, how old and spent, before the Eight Flyers had come. He felt it all again now—only more so in the presence of these vibrant, shining people. A great longing suddenly grew up in him to rest, to sell his tools and move with Anna into the retirement house next door and spend his days holding her hand in the sun. He had done enough, hadn't he? What child in the Black Forest had cause to complain of his service?

No one tried to rush Klaus in his decision. No one tried to convince him one way or the other. But the whole room seemed to hold its breath.

"I'm tired," Klaus said at last.

Even though they were Saints, the others at the table couldn't quite disguise their disappointment. "Ah," said Saint Nicholas.

"I see," said Saint Farouk.

"Well, it's understandable," said Saint Babukar.

Saint Abigail just waited, smiling a small, knowing smile.

"So I'm going to sleep for a week before I start making next year's toys," Klaus said. He looked at the relieved faces all around the table. "You didn't really think I would quit, did you?"

The room breathed again. "Klaus will continue his work," Nicholas intoned solemnly, just as though he was proclaiming Klaus's decision for some official record.

Babukar slapped Klaus heartily on the back. "I knew you would make the right choice!" he said.

"All Animal Creation rejoices!" Farouk said happily. "The eagle on his crag and leviathan in the deep. The leopard as he paces the forest and the camel as he—"

"Camels never rejoice," interrupted Babukar. "This I know from my own experience."

"Perhaps you were not good to your camels, you and the other kings!" Farouk replied tartly. "Perhaps you were not so wise when it came to care of humps and feet!"

Babukar was about to retort, but Klaus intervened hastily. "If the Green Council is really serious about helping," he said, "more villages are added to my list each year.

Even with flying reindeer it's a large job. I could use some assistance with my deliveries."

Saint Farouk looked pale. "I am uncomfortable with heights," he announced.

"My back is not what it was," Babukar noted.

"We have other help to give, Klaus," said Saint Nicholas. "We come with certain gifts. And because you have chosen to continue your work, we may now bestow them. And the first gift is, both you and Anna are to Tarry."

"As are the reindeer!" said Farouk excitedly. "As representatives of the Animal Creation!"

"None of you is to grow an hour older, and death will never take you so long as your task lasts," said Nicholas. "It's a great honor, Tarrying. But you will not do it here. Your work will continue elsewhere."

"And then, of course, you're both to be made Saints," said Babukar. "Like us."

"And the reindeer!" said Farouk enthusiastically.

Nicholas gave Farouk a hard look. "No, not the reindeer. Animals, no matter how admirable, cannot be made Saints."

"What about the Lamb of God?" replied Farouk.

"It's a metaphor!" Babukar said. "Everyone knows that!"

"I'm not so sure," Farouk said. "Speaking as a shepherd, I can definitely say that sheep rank at the very pinnacle of Creation."

"Sheep?" Babukar protested. "They are dumber than camels!"

"But," asked Anna in some discomfort, "don't people pray to Saints? I don't think I'd like that."

"Oh, that's nothing to worry about," Nicholas said. "All prayers really go to God. You won't even hear them."

"Klaus will." They all turned to see Abigail standing with shining eyes that seemed to see beyond the walls of the big room within the small room. "One day, from all over the world, will come to Klaus the petitions of children." Then she turned and looked at Anna. "You have longed for children, dear heart." Anna gasped. How did she know? "So," Abigail continued, "all the children in the world everywhere and forever now belong to you and Klaus. You are Mother and Father Christmas." And Anna's secret sorrow rose up and turned into joy and filled her soul. Neither she nor Klaus comprehended the size of the world nor the number of children in it, but from that hour Anna's thoughts and feelings were ever turned toward them.

Saint Nicholas produced a large, very thick roll of

papers and thumped it onto the table. "Now," he said, "we have many plans to deliberate before we bestow our gifts."

Babukar yawned extravagantly. "Enough!" he said. "The stars come out soon. I must watch them."

"Always you think of your stars!" Farouk grumbled. "Why do you not regard Creation here on earth? You take sheep, for instance—"

"I will not take sheep!" roared Babukar. "Keep your sheep to yourself! I want nothing to do with them!"

"Gentlemen," said Nicholas, "we have important matters to discuss." He started to unroll his papers. "Klaus, Anna—"

Abigail put a hand on Nicholas's arm. "Do you not think their hearts will tell them all they really need to know?"

"Ah!" Babukar said, again holding up one of his ebony fingers. "That will make their lives interesting instead of boring."

Nicholas thought for a moment. "Yes," he said slowly. "I see that you are right." Then he used his intoning voice again. "Klaus and Anna will not be told. They will discover their new lives moment by moment." He stood up from the table. "Will someone fetch the reindeer, please?" he asked.

Anna went outside and whistled for Dasher, and he came trotting up with his brothers and sister. When the reindeer entered the room it expanded even more to accommodate the bigger crowd. The reindeer showed not the least glimmer of surprise at this; nor at being in the presence of Saints; nor, when it was explained to them, what was about to happen. "This is what we were born for," Dasher said simply.

"You see!" said Saint Farouk. "Animals always know. And remember, reindeer are closely related to sheep! Very closely! Are you certain, Nicholas, that we cannot make them Saints, as well?"

Nicholas assured Farouk that Tarrying would be honor enough, and Babukar questioned the consanguinity of sheep to reindeer, and Farouk launched into a learned discourse on Animal Creation, its Orders and Families. But eventually the table and all but two of the thrones were moved aside. Anna and Klaus sat on the remaining thrones side by side, holding hands, in the middle of the room. The reindeer stood close all around them.

Then Nicholas cleared his throat and announced, "Because Klaus has chosen freely to continue his work, it is given to us to bestow on you all the gift of Tarrying. And so

I say to all of you, Tarry. And Klaus and Anna, you are now Saints. Saint Anna and Saint Klaus."

A ripple of influence went out from Nicholas and the other Saints, and with it the delicious scent of peppermint, which by now you must know is the odor of Christmas Magic. The ripple passed into those in the center of the circle like an effervescence that stirred their blood and made them feel so awake that they wondered if they had spent their former lives half asleep. Anna and Klaus sprang to their feet.

And then the ripple rebounded back from them, past the Saints, out of the house, and into the village. All the men in the retirement house next door sniffed that peppermint scent and abruptly felt like getting out their tools and starting a project. Farmers suddenly found they could hardly wait to start their spring planting, and mothers took needle and thread and contemplated darning a hundred pairs of socks. Even a fussy baby in the house farthest away in the village stopped crying and said its first words: "Santa Klaus."

But the ripple, so energizing to most, had a far different effect on one man. Rolf Eckhof, who had fled after giving Anna poisoned herbs, could not stay away for long. Some men must see the effect of their evil deed to be satisfied, and Rolf Eckhof was of this sort. So he had crept back to the house and loitered in the shadows to see if his revenge against Klaus, so long planned, had taken effect. Was the woman dead or not? It was the only Christmas gift he wanted, and he was sick with the desire of it. He had to know.

Rolf Eckhof was in the very act of climbing stealthily in through the bedroom window when the ripple struck him. And because he was so ravaged by malice and deceit—and now murder—it destroyed his body entirely. Not a particle of it was ever found. And it flung his poor, shredded immortal soul to the four winds.

It was long, long years before he was able to reassemble that dark spirit and make more trouble for Klaus. But of course he did. And the trouble he caused was so demonic—for that is what he was now, a demon—that it may yet engulf us all.

But knowing nothing of any of this, Anna and Klaus looked at each other and saw that they were changed. Their hair—and Klaus's beard—were now pure snow white. Yet looking into Anna's eyes, Klaus could see that down in her soul she was young and wild as springtime—and somehow deeply and more truly Anna than ever before in her life.

Anna meanwhile took one look at the reindeer and knew exactly what was about to happen. "Cover your ears!" she shouted. And they all did, just in time. Because Dasher and his brothers and sister lifted up their heads and opened their mouths and bugled so loud that the rafters actually shook. Anna suddenly wondered why she had not gone racing with Dasher for so many years, and Klaus bet any man or beast in the room that he could run to the top of Mount Feldberg without stopping. Nobody took his bet.

Then Klaus gathered his woodworking tools and his crimson coat and breeches, and Anna her fabrics and sewing things, and together they loaded them all into the sleigh. These were the only things they wanted to take with them from their old life.

"Take your cookstove, Anna!" Saint Nicholas advised. "Of all your fine cookery, my dear, which dish is your favorite?"

"My maple sugar cookies," she said automatically. "Naturally."

"Hear, hear!" agreed Klaus.

"Very well then," said Nicholas. "From this day forward,

Klaus, all cookies will do you good, but specially Anna's maple sugar cookies. They will renew you, body and spirit. Please eat a lot of them. If you do, you will find yourself growing ever stronger as the years roll by." And so they loaded the cookstove onto the sleigh with the other things.

Klaus wrote a brief letter to the retired Guild members next door, bequeathing to them his and Anna's house. Before he sealed it, he included in the letter the key to the house and some recipes Anna knew they particularly liked. Klaus slipped the letter quietly inside the front door of the retirement home, then stood arm in arm with Anna gazing at their own cottage. "We have been happy here for thirty-one years," Anna said to Klaus. They both cried a little to honor their house, and then they left.

Led by Nicholas, the Eight Flyers pulled their sleigh deep into the loneliest part of the Black Forest. There waiting for them was a broad shining ice Road, its entrance marked on either side by two variegated holly bushes in silver pots, each engraved with a star and a reindeer rampant. It ran steeply up until it disappeared into the clouds. The Magic scent of peppermint filled the air.

"Here is your first discovery, Klaus," Nicholas told him. "This is the Straight Road."

"This world and all its roads are curved," Farouk explained. "Only this Road is straight and can lead you to your new home." And so it was. In that far-off year of Klaus's transformation and for many years thereafter, the Straight Road was fixed permanently to the earth in that remote region of the Black Forest. Alas for our days when it can no longer be so!

The Green Council bid Klaus and the others farewell. "We will come if you need us," Abigail said.

"But don't call frivolously!" Babukar said. "I will be very busy watching the stars!"

Farewells were said, and then the Eight Flyers bounded up the precipitous expanse of the Straight Road. Anna stood up on the bench of the sleigh and stretched her arms wide, exulting in the frigid wind on her face. She hadn't had so much fun since she was a girl. "Faster, Dasher, faster!" she called out, just as she had of old. And Dasher complied, redoubling the speed of his team. Anna briefly lost her balance, regained it, and whooped for joy. Klaus grinned at her delight. On the reindeer ran, up through the clouds and then still farther, until the circles of this world dropped away and they came at last to the True North.

A long time that country had been preparing for them, and now it was finished. Merry were its flowery meadows in the budding springtime, cool and bracing its waterfall and lake in high summer, and majestic its dark and spicy pine forests in deep winter. But most beautiful at all times of year was Castle Noël with its magnificent towers and spacious halls of green and silver and pearl. When Klaus first saw it, he knew it was his dream come to real life.

And when he and Anna drove at last through the great crystal gates into the courtyard of that castle and came to a stop, they made their second discovery. A throng of people, hundreds of them, were silently waiting for them there. Anna, a little breathless from the rush of their journey, leaned over to Klaus and whispered in his ear, "Who are they all?"

Then one of the people stepped forward to speak.

CHAPTER FIVE

Of Space and Time

Saint Klaus sat in his sleigh on Christmas Eve and worried. The Eight Flyers stood in their traces. They were puzzled, eager to be in the air again, but they waited patiently. The dawn was coming. Man and beast could feel it—the chill wind blowing up, the dark beginning to thin into gray just at the horizon's edge. Only Dasher had an idea what Klaus was feeling, because his bond with him was so strong and deep. He craned his head around from the front of the line, wanting to say something encouraging, but, seeing

Klaus's expression, could find no suitable words. *Poor man,* he thought. *Whatever will he do now that he realizes?*

It had all gone so well at first. Klaus thought back to his very first day at Castle Noël, when Anna had whispered her question into his ear about the crowd of people in the courtyard: "Who are they all?"

A young woman had stepped forward. Or was she young? Klaus had wondered. She had the freshness of youth but also the completeness of maturity. She may even have been old once, but not now. "Welcome," the young woman had said. "We hope you like your country as much as we have enjoyed making it."

"We like it very much," Klaus had replied. He bowed. "Thank you—all of you—for your labors." The multitude seemed to expect something more from him, but he was unsure what to say next.

Anna noticed the slight glow coming from the throng. "Are you Saints, like Nicholas and the others?" she asked, and added a little hesitantly, "And, well, like us, I suppose."

A murmur of appreciation swept through the crowd in the courtyard. "It's very good of you to say so," the young woman answered with a smile. "Someday, perhaps."

"Then may we know who you are?" Anna asked.

"We're Elevated Spirits, of course!" a man called out.

"You don't *seem* like spirits," Klaus said. "You're all very solid."

"So are all Spirits who have Elevated," another explained.

"Oh, just call us Elves!" someone else said. "That's what we call ourselves!"

"Ah," said Klaus. "Elves. Good." Another expectant pause. *They seem to want something from us*, Klaus thought. *But what?*

Seeing his bewilderment, the young woman spoke low in his ear. "What we all wish to know is, may we stay and help?"

Now Klaus understood! A smile wreathed his face, and he stepped forward and spread his arms wide. "O excellent Elves," he called out in his largest voice, "will you please stay here with us and help Anna and me in our labors?"

At this a great cheer went up from the crowd, and those who had caps threw them in the air. "Three cheers for Saint Klaus and Saint Anna!" they all cried. "And three more for the Eight Flyers who brought them Home!"

All of the Elevated Spirits chose to stay in the new country they had made, and many more who had the desire to make toys came afterwards. "And what if some of the Elves are all thumbs?" Klaus remarked to Anna later. "They can't hurt themselves, being Elevated, and I like teaching them. Besides, we're going to need the help. I have a feeling our deliveries are going to expand."

And expand they had. Each Christmas Eve, Klaus had driven down the Straight Road with more and bigger sacks of toys. And always, no matter how far afield Klaus had flown, his fame had flown faster, and more and more children had waited in eager expectation for his visits.

On their very first Christmas Eve in the True North, Klaus and Anna had stood, as they usually did, beside their big sleigh, loaded and ready to depart. Only now the sleigh was not beside their snug cottage, but in the courtyard of Castle Noël. Dasher and his siblings stood in their traces, patiently waiting, one or another of them quietly shifting a hoof now and then. Only someone who knew them well would have noticed the barely perceptible electric shiver all along their splendid silver coats, the hallmark of their eagerness to be off and away. Elves thronged the courtyard or were up in the balconies of the castle, ready to cheer when the sleigh shot away down the Road.

Klaus turned to Anna. "Well, my dear," he said and

held out a mittened hand. "Shall I help you—" He was about to say, "into the sleigh," but he caught the expression on her face and said instead, in some alarm, "Anna! Whatever is wrong?"

"Not a thing," Anna replied as quickly as she could.

But it was too late. Perhaps because Klaus was now a Saint and that made him more perceptive, he saw what for thirty-one Christmas Eves he had failed to see: a slight frown passing fleetingly across his wife's face. "Now, Anna," Klaus said, taking her hands, "I have seen your face merry, fierce, sad, and very, very occasionally, in repose. But I have never seen *that* expression on it before. It seems to say—it seems to signify—Anna, are you *irritated* with me?"

"Of course not! Oh, Klaus, dear, dear Klaus, I never meant for you to see! I never meant for you to know." Anna was on the very brink of tears. *And that is something new, too*, Klaus thought, marveling.

"Know what?" he asked. Anna glanced at the Elves looking curiously at them and wondering what was transpiring. Klaus followed her gaze. "Good Elevated Spirits," Klaus called out, "will you be so kind as to give my wife and me a moment?" The Elves made polite noises and backed a respectful distance away. "Now then, Anna, won't you please, *please* tell me what is troubling you? What was I never meant to know?"

Well, Anna could see that there was nothing for it now but to confess. And so she did. And it would, according to her later report, be untrue to say that her voice did not catch once or twice as she poured out her heart to her husband. Halfway through she heard Klaus murmur to himself, "All those years! How could I not have seen it?" And she saw the complete astonishment on his face when, after she was entirely finished, he turned to her and said, "But still, Anna, it's really very hard to believe. You say you find delivering Christmas presents *boring?*"

Anna nodded through her tears. "Tedious beyond belief," she sobbed. How good it felt finally to say it! "I've tried to like it for your sake, but—all those houses, more each year! And me waiting while you check off each toy on all your bits of paper, and then waiting some more while you let them down the chimney. I hate waiting! I hate doing the same thing again and again! I know you like my company—and I treasure yours, too, Klaus, on all other occasions—and I never wanted to hurt your feelings, but the truth is—I don't like going out with you on Christmas Eve." It was the most terrible thing Anna had ever said to anyone, and she had just said it to the person she cared most about in all the world. What, she wondered desperately, would come of it?

Klaus was stunned. He wondered how he could have been so blind to his wife's feelings for so long. And he was worried: *How will it be not to have her beside me on the most important night of the year?* He could not speak for several moments while Anna stood by in agony. And then, unexpectedly, a new understanding came to him like a dove settling on his heart. "It is another discovery," he said at last.

"What is?" Anna asked.

"Why, that happiness is the result when the truth is spoken in love. Anna, you have given me a great gift this Christmas Eve. I thank you." And he actually bowed to her.

"Don't make me cry again," Anna said gruffly. "I already feel like such a *girl*! Especially in front of the reindeer."

"Ho, ho, ho! Then laugh with me, instead!" said Klaus. And she did, because who can resist that laugh? "Now I will give *you* a gift. You will never, *ever* have to come with me again on Christmas Eve!"

Anna clapped her hands with glee. "Really? Oh, Klaus, it's the best present you ever gave me!"

And so it was that thereafter Klaus made his Christmas

Eve flights without Anna. And while it was true that they grew lonely and missed each other when they were apart, it was also true that they came to know the deep pleasure of returning to each other and eagerly sharing all their doings when they came back together. For them, as they have often said, it is the very best way to live. And Anna, as will be seen, was seldom idle while her husband was away.

On that first Christmas Eve in the True North, Klaus gave his wife a lingering hug, jumped into his sleigh, and held on while his reindeer (*Finally!* they thought) thundered out of the courtyard, down the Straight Road, and off to make their deliveries. Anna joined the Elves in cheering and waving as they shot through the castle gates.

And then the glad years had taken wing, one after the other, and flown away. How many years? It was hard to count them in the True North. You will get an idea of life there if you think of being on holiday. When you are on holiday, you fill each precious day with just what you like to do and with just whom you want to do it, and you love each day just for itself. You don't really care if it's Tuesday or Friday, and you are freed from the noise and bother of the world so long as your holiday lasts. Well, in the True North, the holiday always lasts.

And so while Klaus noticed that the chimneys he let

toys down were beginning to be made of brick and this made his job longer and trickier, and while Anna noted that her batches of maple sugar cookies, enjoyed by one and all at Castle Noël, were growing ever larger, and while Dasher made meticulous mental notes of all the new places they were visiting and, with the help of cartographer Elves, converted his observations into more and more maps and flight charts, none of them could tell you exactly how many years had passed since the founding of the True North, nor could any tell you exactly what year it was as reckoned by earthly calendars. They were, you see, all on holiday.

But now, brooding in his sleigh on this particular Christmas Eve some years later, Klaus felt that all his happiness had evaporated. The dawn was coming. Man and beast could feel it—the chill wind blowing up, the dark beginning to thin into gray just at the horizon's edge. And though he was too far away to hear it, he knew the matins bell would soon be ringing out in his little former village, signaling the end of Christmas Eve—and the end of the blessing Father Goswin had invoked all those years ago on toys delivered on this special night. He looked behind him

in the sleigh and saw amid all the empty sacks the one still
half-filled with toys for what was intended to be the last
village of the night—and the first where the children
spoke an entirely different language. Now those children
would be disappointed. He had stretched his route too far.
It was now impossible, even for a flying Saint, to make all
his deliveries on Christmas Eve. He had failed.

Klaus sighed. He reached for the reins to turn the team
back toward the Straight Road when from the front of the
line he heard a word.

"Try" was the word. Klaus looked up from his brooding. Dasher was looking hard at him. "Try," the reindeer
said again. "It is not yet dawn, Klaus. Remember what
Saint Nicholas said. There may still be more for us to discover. Try."

Well. There was never harm in trying. In fact, come to
think of it, Klaus thought, trying was itself a kind of Magic.
All right. He would try, despite the gray turning into rose
just at the eastern horizon's edge behind him. "Very well!"
he shouted. "On, Dasher! On, Dancer! And, oh, on, everyone!" The Eight Flyers sprang up, filling the air with the
silver jingle of their harness bells as they flew away.

Maybe, hoped Klaus as the wind whistled through his
beard, *if I don't look behind me, I can pretend the sun isn't*

rising. If I just keep going, perhaps I can—somehow—get to that foreign village before it's too late. He shut his eyes tight against the morning light he feared was coming. (Luckily, Dasher was carrying a good map of Europe in his head, so Klaus didn't need to steer.) *If only the dawn wouldn't come!* Klaus wished. And then he said aloud with all his heart, "If only Time would stop!"

Except that he didn't say that, at all. The sleigh was just at that moment shooting over the border into the new country and so what Klaus actually said was, *"Si seulement le Temps s'arrêterait!"* It so astonished him to find himself speaking another language that he opened his eyes.

And then he wished he had not. For looming up suddenly in front of the sleigh was a vast wall of what looked like ice, all sapphire and emerald and amethyst. *"Attention!"* shouted Klaus. But it was no good. The wall had appeared so fast that Dasher in the lead knew he couldn't avoid crashing into it. He braced for a collision that he knew would break all their bones and shatter the sleigh to pieces. The team hit the wall with the speed of a comet and—simply passed through. It was not ice at all. It was a piece of the Aurora Borealis, flown down from the north and dancing in the air in front of them. First Dasher and Dancer and then all the reindeer and last of all Klaus in the sleigh passed into the Northern Lights and out the other side. They all felt a shimmer of warmth, as though they had gone through a band of summer, and caught the scent of peppermint that let them know they were in the presence of Christmas Magic.

Dasher led the sleigh down from the clouds onto the ground and slid to a stop. They all needed to catch their breaths and let their hearts slow down. Each made a check of his or her body parts. Yes, thank goodness, all still knit together in one piece.

Then suddenly Klaus groaned. He had just remembered the village and the toys. "Now we are even later!" he said, only he said it in the new language, which the reindeer now understood perfectly. "We will never get the toys to the last village before—" He looked back over his shoulder to the dawn that must surely be growing in the east. And then the words simply died on his lips. The dawn was not growing. The sky was not one scintilla lighter or pinker than it had been before they had passed through the Aurora. The sun was stuck. Time had stopped.

Klaus and the Eight Flyers looked out at the world in amazement. Nothing moved. Not the clouds partially obscuring the winter stars, not a single blade of the gray grass poking through the crust of snow at their feet. A fox on the hunt a little distance away looked as though he were pasted to the ground, with one paw up. The world was motionless and silent. Finally, after no one said anything for a rather long time, Klaus ventured in a voice hushed with wonder, "We shall have to be careful about birds when we're flying."

And so, just as Saint Nicholas had said he would, Klaus had discovered still another important piece of his life's work: the art and science of Chronolepsy. Or, as the Elvish slang has it, Time Stop. On Christmas Eve—and only on Christmas Eve—Klaus may call on Time to Tarry as he Tarries. A flame of the Aurora Borealis rushes to him wherever he is and bathes him, his sleigh, and the Eight Flyers in its dancing light, and then they may take as long as they wish with their deliveries. They may fly for days or months while Time takes a holiday.

To those in the world, of course, Time does not stop, and so to them it appears that Klaus's work takes no time at all. Toys are simply there, under the tree or in stockings on Christmas morning. Only a very special person, one who is almost an Elevated Spirit already, may see Klaus or his reindeer on Christmas Eve—and then only as the barest flicker that teases their imaginings. Charles Dickens was such a person, as were Clement Moore and Mr. May—but once again I'm getting ahead of this chronicle.

On this memorable Christmas Eve the Eight flew to the last village and, for the first time in his life, Klaus delivered his toys without the least worry about how long it was taking. But he also found some houses that had no chimneys or smoke holes at all, just small pipes in their roofs. And so he was forced to put his toys by the sides of doors, as he had done of old—which had led, he remembered uncomfortably, to Rolf Eckhof's thefts.

When all the deliveries had been made, a novel and enticing idea came into Klaus's head. "It's been a long night, I know," he said to Dasher and the others. "Still, I wonder if anyone might care to, well, to see something of the world. Time must be stopped at Castle Noël, too, so there's no need to hurry back." And then all his eagerness came tumbling out. "I've heard there's an ocean and I want to see if it's true! And are there really places where there's always snow—and places where there's never?"

Well, you know how it is with Klaus's enthusiasms. It's best not to stand too close when they occur, because they're as catching as a cold. Vixen, who *was* standing close, suddenly had a fleeting vision of sweet grass under swaying trees that made her pretty ears stand straight up. That same vision hit Comet and Blitzen next, and they stamped their hoofs twice each. By the time it arrived at Dasher and Dancer in the front of the traces, all the reindeer were snorting steam and pawing the snow, restless to be off on their tour. Dasher bugled to the sky. Then he cried in a great voice, "Let us show this carpenter what it means to really fly!" And they sprang from the roof with such a violence of speed that Klaus nearly fell out of his sleigh. Within a few seconds they were streaking north faster than a shooting star.

"We will take you to our home first!" Dasher shouted back to Klaus. And under half an hour later the sleigh swooped low and Klaus marveled at what he saw: ten thousand reindeer spread across a vast field of snow glowing faintly periwinkle in the light of the predawn sun. And though the reindeer, too, were Chronoleptically stuck, their antlered heads were all pointing south. "They go to better pasturage," Prancer told Klaus. Except what he really said was, *"Ne menevät paremmin laitumelle,"* because that was how people spoke where they were now. It was really quite wonderful, this phenomenon of languages coming into your head the moment you entered the countries in which they were spoken. Like Chronolepsy, it occurs only on Christmas Eve, and came to be known at Castle Noël as the Lingua Franca Effect. It is, incidentally, this Effect, distilled and infused into its pages, which allows you and everyone else in the world, Esteemed Reader, to understand this book.

Then Dasher led the sleigh up and away. They flew east now, even faster than before, and much higher. In fact they were soon at such a prodigious altitude that most people would not have found air or heat enough to sustain them, but they were not troubled by this. As they reached the very pinnacle of the sky, Klaus beheld the curve of the earth and then he knew the true purpose of his strong desire. He had been meant to see this sight—the whole world as one mighty arc. *The earth is great beyond my wildest reckoning,* he thought. *And it must contain children beyond count.* For the first time the enormity of the task he had volunteered to undertake became clear to him, and it left him hushed and humbled. To make toys and deliver them to all those children: the thought was staggering.

They flew and flew, across broad plains and dark blue seas, and the languages that jumped into and out of their heads one after another grew dizzying. They passed over vast deserts and steppes of tall grass. And still they flew. Klaus munched one or two of Anna's cookies. They sustained him wonderfully, and he felt he had the energy to go on forever, but the reindeer were getting a little hungry.

In time, Klaus and the Eight came to a range of mountains so lofty that, high as they were flying, the eternally white peak of the tallest almost scraped the runners of the sleigh as they hurtled past it. By this time the sun, still fastened immovably in the sky, was directly overhead. Far down below, Klaus spied what looked like a huge fortress in a mountain fastness. "Dasher!" he called. "Let's get a closer look." So Dasher wheeled and turned and sped down the sky toward the big complex of buildings. The walls of it grew from the very rock. They slowed and flew closer to peer into the courtyards. There they saw golden men in saffron robes, all Chronoleptically stopped in mid-motion. But one man was completely unaffected. He was looking up at them and waving cheerfully. "Come down!" he called to Klaus. "There is provender for your reindeer, and I would like some conversation with you!"

While Dasher and his siblings munched on hay—and it was foreign and spicy but very good—Klaus walked in a bright courtyard with the man who had hailed him. Kelzang Gyatso was his name. And if any had been there to observe, they would have smiled to see two such different men walking together, one large and clad in crimson with great boots on his feet, the other slight, barefoot, and wearing a yellow robe—and yet, somehow they went together. Kelzang told Klaus about Four Noble Truths and an Eightfold Path, and it all seemed very beautiful, if strange, to Klaus. At last Kelzang said, "Well, Klaus, you have seen the world now and seen it whole. What do you think of it?"

"Some children must be poor," Klaus said, "even 'hungry."

"That is true," Kelzang replied.

"I do not like the thought," Klaus said.

"You are one who is called to relieve the *dukkha*—the sorrow of the world—through your Christmas labors," Kelzang said. "You are a fire, Klaus, and if any will draw near you with their hearts, they will be kindled by you, and they will feed the hungry children."

That gladdened Klaus, but there was one more nagging problem.

"It may seem trivial compared to all we have discussed, but . . ."

"Go on, please," Kelzang said.

"How am I to get toys inside of homes," Klaus blurted out, "now that I see that many have no chimneys?"

"Ah, I see," said Kelzang. "Come with me please." Looking up from his munching, Dasher saw Klaus and the man in the saffron robe disappear into a building with a golden door. When they came out, half an hour later, he heard Kelzang say to Klaus, "I think you will find it to be useful."

"Well?" Dasher asked Klaus as they prepared to fly away. "What did he show you?"

"Wait and see!" Klaus said. There was a distinct twinkle in his eye.

In a moment they were once more flying high over great, wide plains, and then across a narrow sea to another land. "*Sagarimasu, kudasai!*" Klaus called out as they approached a city of graceful upturned tile roofs, and Dasher obliged by flying lower. "I have one more gift to give this Christmas Eve!" he said. In a moment they were beside a particular house Klaus had chosen.

"But there is no chimney," Dasher said.

"Precisely," said Klaus as he rummaged around to find the last toy in his sack, a set of paints and brushes. He stood before the house's very solid, very locked door and shut his eyes. Privately Dasher wondered if perhaps his old friend was light-headed from all the high-altitude flying. "This door is an illusion," Klaus murmured. "It is *maya*, a veil through which I may pass." And then Klaus walked through the closed door as if it were not there.

The reindeer shot sixty feet into the air in surprise. But

almost before they had returned to earth, Klaus was outside the house again, rubbing his hands in glee. "Well, well," he said. "It works! Just as Kelzang said it would! I don't understand a bit of it, but it works! I never have to worry about chimneys again!"

And so, the Maya Principle was born. It is this: No closed door, no wall no matter its thickness, may keep Klaus out on Christmas Eve. He has always credited this phenomenon to the teaching of Kelzang Gyatso. But as Dasher muttered while Klaus cheerfully climbed back into the sleigh and they all shot once more into the sky, "Comes from being a Saint, I suppose."

The little boy who received the paint set, by the way, was called Tokitaro, and it launched him on a great and distinguished art career.

And now Klaus and the Eight were speeding east over an immense azure ocean, bigger than anything they had yet encountered. The sun was behind them when they finally spotted a chain of islands like jewels sparkling in the sea. The language that entered their heads now was all soft breezes and the gentle roll of waves on white sand. Without any warning at all Vixen suddenly plunged down out of the air, dragging all the other reindeer and the sleigh with her.

"*Akahele!*" Klaus shouted in alarm, but it was no good. The vision of soft grass under swaying trees had abruptly entered Vixen's head again, and she felt certain its fulfillment was below. Sure enough, when they landed on one of the islands—it had a volcano right in the middle of it—they found bright, tender grass under trees unlike anything they had ever seen before, with bare trunks and leaves like banners radiating in a circle from the top.

Acting on a hunch, Klaus called out, "Time start!" Immediately the strange trees began to sway in a gentle breeze, the stream over which they hung began to flow, and nearby, azure waves broke on a sandy beach. "So that works," Klaus said to Dasher. He had just made the penultimate discovery of that most memorable Christmas Eve. Chronoleptic Oscillation (as the physicists of the True North call it) allows Klaus to stop and start Time precisely as he moves across the globe so that his deliveries all take place on Christmas Eve, wherever in the world he may be.

But what the reindeer—especially Vixen—really cared about at the moment was the grass. All agreed after the first bite that it was the tenderest, freshest any of them had ever eaten. Encouraged by this, Klaus tried a sweet, pulpy orange fruit he picked from a tree nearby and found it delicious. He followed it with a large, hard nut, which, when cracked on a runner of the sleigh, revealed snow white meat and a refreshing drink. Then he took off as many of his clothes as he thought proper—and I do not know, because he has not said, how many that was—and splashed into the sea. The reindeer followed his lead, and they all had a glorious time swimming in the surf after their long labors and a longer flight. And if you have never seen a reindeer bodysurf, I must tell you that you have missed an astonishing sight. "What a shame Anna has missed this!" Klaus declared as he and the Eight rinsed the salt water off in the stream and dried themselves in the tropical sun. "But I shall bring her here on a holiday next Christmas Eve while Time is still stopped." And that is exactly what he did—and has done most every Christmas Eve since.

Then they flew away into the east until they came once again to countries where it was still night, and then on to where it was just beginning to be dawn. The language in Klaus's head was now his own, and he knew he was back where he had started. So if anyone asks you, Esteemed Reader, who was the first to circumnavigate the globe, you now have the answer.

The Straight Road shone in front of Klaus and the Eight, a beacon in the Black Forest. All were eager to race up it at once and away home, but something caught Klaus's eye: the final discovery of the night. A piece of paper folded twice was lodged in the left-hand holly bush standing at the entrance. Klaus stooped to pluck it from the branches. He read it once, and then he read it through carefully again. "Oh my," he said. He tucked it into his pocket as the sleigh sped up the Road.

"Time start!" he shouted as Castle Noël came into sight. Everything burst into life. By the time they glided to a stop in the courtyard, the sun was up. A door opened and Anna ran out to greet Klaus. "Welcome home!" she said. And then she stepped back and looked suspiciously at her husband in the dawn light. "How did you manage to get a suntan on Christmas Eve?" she asked.

"Never mind that," Klaus said. "Look at this!" And he gave her the folded note. When she read it, her eyes grew wide. "Oh my," she said.

"I know," Klaus said. "This changes everything."

CHAPTER SIX

Be of Good Cheer

Explanations about the mysterious suntan Klaus had acquired would have to wait. That is what Anna thought as she eyed her Saintly husband's healthy glow, though she did wonder what he had been up to and if he had been having fun without her. And Klaus thought, *Wait till she hears about Time stopping! And about all those languages and how big the world is, and no more need to worry about chimneys!*

But what they both thought was, *First things first. What shall we do about this letter left at the foot of the Straight Road?*

The letter was from a child. This is what it said: "Dear Santa, Next Christmas Eve will you please bring me a kite so I can fly it in the summer? I would like it best if it had a picture of a dragon on it, because that is my favorite animal in the world. Very sincerely yours, Sophie. PS: I love you, Santa, and so does my little brother Arnulf, who would like a puppy."

Now, the alarming thing about this letter was not that it was addressed to someone called "Santa." All at Castle Noël knew that this name for Klaus was becoming increasingly popular, since it was—or was near—the word for "Saint." Nor was it alarming that the letter asked for a toy Klaus did not know how to make. For many Christmases now Elves had been making toys based on ideas of their own or Anna's. That is very much the case now, of course, though all toys must still be personally approved by Klaus.

No, the truly troubling thing about the letter was simply that Sophie *had asked for a specific gift*—which had never happened before. Oh, Klaus had sometimes made a toy specially for a child—remember little Lena's rattle? But no one had ever written to *ask* for a particular one. You can see the implications of this, I'm sure, as clearly as Anna and Klaus could. What if everyone began asking for specific gifts? Would they be able to honor these requests? Children might ask for anything. Arnulf had asked for a puppy, which neither Klaus nor even the most skilled of the Elves could make. And was little Arnulf ready for a puppy? This last question led them to an even larger one: What if children asked for toys that were not right for them? What should they do then?

Dasher and his siblings declared themselves too tired to pursue these thorny issues at the moment and trotted off to their stables for a long winter's nap, but Klaus and Anna stayed up well into the night sipping mint hot chocolate by the enormous fire in the Great Hall of Castle Noël and trying to decide what was best to do. About the subject of dangerous playthings Anna grew quite excited. She instantly began planning a range of toys that would re-create in full working detail, but in children's sizes, the armor and weapons of the Roman Ninth Legion. "Think what fun my children would have with their own real swords and shields!" Anna exulted, her eyes glowing. "And we could make a line of working catapults! And scale models of Teutonic Heroines on Horseback! I could stitch their outfits myself!" And then Klaus wondered aloud if parents would object to toys that might lead to loss of blood, and Anna declared indignantly that that was all part of a happy childhood. But in the end she reluctantly conceded that decisions about toy safety would probably have to be left up to parents. "Mind you," she grumbled, "I'm sure the children would see it my way." And she returned to her enormous project of stitching all the battles of the Crusades onto Christmas stockings for the Elves.

They talked through the night. And by morning, though they were tremendously sleepy and full of cocoa, they had hammered out the main ideas of what became the famed Christmas List Protocols, and retired to their sleigh bed contented with their work. As Klaus drifted off to sleep, into his mind came the words of Saint Abigail, spoken so many years before: "One day, from all over the world, will come to Klaus the petitions of children." So, he thought, smiling, this was what she had meant.

The three original Protocols, decided that night, were as follows:

1. Children may make written requests to "Santa" Klaus about their Christmas gifts. These will arrive at Castle Noël by Magic.

2. There is no guarantee that an item requested will be delivered. But we will do our best.
3. It is unlikely [We see the hand of Anna in that word, "unlikely"] that a toy will be delivered if it is deemed unsafe or unsuitable by a child's parent or guardian.

These original Protocols were posted at the foot of the Straight Road with the conviction that Sophie and Arnulf would spread the word. Given the volume of requests that poured into Castle Noël the next year and the steady increase for many years thereafter, we may safely assume that is exactly what happened.

I am sorry to have to report, however, that these three simple and commonsense Protocols have had to be much amended over the years, due to changing conditions and misunderstandings in the world. So long as the Straight Road remained tethered to the earth, these additions to the original Protocols were posted periodically at its foot. But when that tie was broken, they had to be communicated, imperfectly I am afraid, through dreams and bursts of inspiration to sensitive souls on earth, generally on Christmas Eve. Unfortunately, this means of transmission has inevitably led to distortions of the Protocols. However, on the plus side, it has also resulted in many a jolly, if inaccurate, story or song about how to behave when "Santa Claus is coming to town," the correct attitude to adopt in the unlikely event of seeing "Mommy kissing Santa Claus," etc. Around Castle Noël, these always get a good laugh.

However, to set the record straight, all the List Protocols are reproduced in Appendix H of this *Green Book*, precisely as they appear in the striking tapestries woven by Anna that hang in the Gifts Pavilion by Advent Lake in the True North. Here, for a sample, I set down just three of the more recent amendments:

237. Gift requests must be made in writing. Castle Noël is a house of order and keeps records. Accordingly, a child speaking his or her requests to someone in a commercial emporium dressed up in a costume vaguely imitative of the traveling suit originally made by Anna for Klaus will NOT constitute a valid Christmas list. Please write it down.

238. Each child may make his or her list of requests as long as he or she pleases. Santa will be happy to consider the first three items. After that his attention tends to flag.

239. It has come to our attention that for very valid reasons some parent or guardian at some time may wish to give a

child a Christmas gift and say it is from Santa. Hence, we have drawn up the Great Pact, which states: Any gift given in love in Santa's name will be deemed to be given by Santa. Further, Santa will pass by without delivering to any house participating in the Great Pact. Finally, any person who gives a surrogate Santa gift will automatically be considered signatory to the Great Pact, in perpetuity. Please apply in person if you wish to have this action reversed. [A holograph facsimile of the Great Pact, signed by Klaus and Anna and hoofmarked by each of the Eight Flyers, can also be found in Appendix h.]

Once the original Protocols were devised, Klaus and Anna and all the Elves began to think of their toy making in a new way. And in this Anna was the leader. For it was her ingenious innovations that brought the True North into what we historians consider the Modern Epoch*—although it began simply as Anna indulging her taste for adventure.

As soon as Anna heard about Chronolepsy, she laid her plans. And the very next Christmas Eve, for the first time

*Some scholars mark the beginning of the Modern Epoch as the day when Anna consulted some particularly deep-thinking Elves. "In a Christmas Eve

in a long time, she was back beside Klaus in his sleigh—but not for very long. For as soon as Klaus called out "Time Stop!" and they all plunged through the dancing lights of the Aurora Borealis, Anna leapt from the sleigh directly onto the back of Donner—who had agreed to be her accomplice—and unhitched him from his traces. "See you when you get back, husband!" she yelled over her shoulder to Klaus as she and the reindeer raced back up the Straight Road. Klaus gazed fondly at her swiftly retreating back. "After all, Dasher," he said, "why should I have all the fun?" Secretly, Dasher wished he were going with his old racing companion instead of Donner, but he knew he could not be spared from leading the team.

And so, while Klaus made his deliveries that year, Anna and Donner made an intrepid expedition into the mighty

---

or two, my husband's sleigh will no longer hold all the toys he must deliver," she told them when they assembled at Castle Noël. "What shall we do?" The thinkers looked thoughtful. A few stroked their chins. And then one snapped his fingers. "Of course!" he said. "You just leave this to us!" And thus Gift Displacement began. It works this way: All the toys Klaus delivers on a given Christmas Eve are in his large sack on the sleigh, but the inside of the sack is not, strictly speaking, there. It is Somewhere Else: a vast store-room where that year's gifts are all carefully inventoried by the prodigious Sack Staff and organized and primed, so that when Klaus reaches into his bag, the proper toy is ready to hand. *It reminds me,* Klaus thought when he first tried out Displacement, *of the room the Green Council brought to our house in the village that was bigger than our living room but still contained in it.* And, indeed, scientists inform me the principle is much the same.

range of mountains far to the west of Castle Noël. There what had begun as merely a trek for sheer fun turned into something more important even than that. For in those mountains—which Anna named the Yuletide Massif—they discovered enormous veins of pure gold.

And that discovery led to a still greater one: Anna found her True North vocation. Oh, she would continue the dangerous and hair-raising adventures she had begun that Christmas. How could she not? She was Anna. (These, incidentally, will be fully recounted in her own memoir, which Anna hopes to complete one day when her labors permit; I may say here, just to give a taste of them, that the first person to reach the summit of Mount Everest was *neither* Tenzing Norgay *nor* Edmund Hillary.) But as she took up the task of converting a gold mine into the practical and charitable activities which now comprise the Castle Noël economy, she uncovered in herself a talent for what to this day she modestly refers to as "helping out where I can," but which Klaus beamingly calls "running the whole show." She invited many Elevated Spirits with a wide variety of unique skills to the True North. Arnulf's request for a puppy prompted the establishment of the Saint Farouk Kennel and Cattery, staffed by Elves skilled in animal husbandry. Sophie's request brought a cadre of engineers who

could fashion ingenious kites—and later miniature loco-
motives, space shuttles, and the like.

Christmas Eve after Christmas Eve, Anna took full ad-
vantage of Chronolepsy to establish the institutions that
today play such a vital role in the True North—all while
Klaus was away. It delighted him to return from a Christmas Eve flight one year to discover that Anna had founded
and staffed the Saint Nicholas Munificence Bank, and another year the Flying Eight Weather and Travel Bureau,
and another the Institute of Toy Prognostication with its
crack, handpicked research team.

And then Klaus and Anna and as many reindeer as
wished to go would fly off to their tropical retreat together
for their well-earned vacation and to catch up on all they
had done while they were apart.

At the risk of inserting too much personal biography, I
will note that this immigration of newcomers to the True
North eventually included Your Humble Author. Saint
Klaus expressed a desire for a scholar to establish the Castle Noël Archives and serve as Court Historian. I had a
smattering of training from my days as a history don at
Exeter College, Oxford, and my application was accepted.
May I simply say that the last hundred and seven years
have been amongst the happiest and most stimulating of

my life? And until the assaults, which I must shortly report, came upon us, the most peaceful, too.

So much of what the world now thinks of as Christmas and its traditions was born in these years. The Christmas letters of children began to be Magically snatched from pillows and mantelpieces and post offices around the world and transported to the vast Receiving Center built hard by Castle Noël. And if grown-ups felt they couldn't write letters to Santa as their children did—though some secretly did—they could send season's greetings to one another in the form of cheery cards. Unconsciously mimicking old, old traditions, Christmas trees and Christmas stockings began to appear in more and more homes. And it was in this period that a famous author caught a fleeting glimpse of Klaus on a Chronoleptic Christmas Eve flight one year. He suddenly felt inspired to write a tale of miserliness and its redemption, featuring, if only he had known it, Klaus himself as his Ghost of Christmas Present. A poet having a similar experience wrote of a Christmas sighting and, though he missed rather badly on Klaus's character and appearance, to the astonishment of everyone at Castle Noël, he somehow got the names of every one of the Eight Flyers right. And the world grew more and more in love with Christmas each year. For a time, anyway. For two or three mortal spans of years.

One day at the height of this Christmas popularity, Dasher ventured out from Castle Noël with Anna on his back. It was high summer and they were on their way to post the latest List Protocols at the foot of the Straight Road. "Care for a little gallop, Anna?" Dasher had asked. Both knew it was a foolish question. In a moment they were racing like the wind down the Road just for the sheer pleasure of speed. Anna's snow-white hair streamed out behind her, and Dasher's silver flanks gleamed in the hot sun. They were not paying strict attention. Velocity and wind and laughter were the only things on their minds.

And that's how it happened.

"Look out!" Anna cried suddenly. A thick gray fog loomed straight ahead. Dasher dug his hoofs into the hard-packed earth of the Road (it was summer, remember, so no ice), but he could not stop in time. He plunged straight into the fog. It was viscous and clammy, and it made his mind reel. In his confusion, it seemed to him that the world dropped away beneath him. He tried to fly but found himself unable to and fell like a stone off the Road. The malevolent wetness followed him to the ground and engulfed him. Anna pitched off Dasher's back as he fell, sailed clear of the heavy damp cloud, and landed with a sickening thud at the foot of a larch tree on the ground below the Road.

Back at Castle Noël, Klaus looked up abruptly from his work. He sensed that something was very wrong. He leaned out a window. "Comet!" he called out anxiously to the fastest of the Eight Flyers.

A few moments later the two were thundering out from Castle Noël toward the Straight Road. They lighted on it with a bang of all four wheels of the light carriage Comet was pulling and sped down its broad track. Klaus urged Comet to go just a bit faster, and the swift reindeer summoned every ounce of speed he could muster. And then, abruptly, Klaus and Comet encountered the impossible: a jagged edge and empty air. The last thirty feet of the Straight Road were gone. They had simply disappeared. Anna and Dasher had missed seeing the precipice because it had been obscured by the gray fog, now nowhere to be seen. Comet nimbly took flight just before his hoof struck the edge and sailed safely to the ground below.

For a moment Klaus just sat in the carriage, transfixed by the carnage of the broken Road, too appalled to move. How could this have happened? Then he heard a low moan and, looking for its source, he saw Anna, inert beneath the larch tree. He ran to her with a cry and, gathering her in his arms, carried her back to the carriage and laid her gently across the seat. "Dasher," she murmured. Klaus looked wildly around, but could not see the reindeer anywhere. "Over there," Anna whispered, gesturing toward the shattered Road. She winced sharply, because that arm was broken, and then fell mercifully into unconsciousness.

And then Klaus saw Dasher, half-covered in rubble. He was lying on his side, one back leg twisted at a sickening angle. In a flash, Klaus was at his side, pulling broken pieces of the Road off him, cradling his head in his lap. "Dasher!" he sobbed, and kissed his face. "We'll get you home, great heart. Don't worry. You'll be all right!" But Dasher could not reply. Nor could he hear what his old friend was saying. His eyes, wide open as though fixed on some terrifying object, were sightless. And his mind was filled with horror.

"It was Rolf Eckhof, of course," said Saint Nicholas.

The Green Council was meeting in the Great Hall of Castle Noël. Anna was there, her arm in a sling, but otherwise none the worse for her harrowing experience. Klaus sat close beside her, his hand on hers.

"But it was . . . it was just a sort of cloud, wasn't it, Anna?" asked Klaus. "That's what you said."

"It never touched me," Anna said. "And yet, I felt such despair, such hopelessness . . ." She shuddered, and Klaus put his arm around her. "I cannot speak of it," she murmured.

Klaus looked up at the Council. "How can a gray cloud be Rolf Eckhof?" he asked.

"I don't know that there is much of Rolf Eckhof left," Saint Abigail said. She sighed. "Mostly there is just a fog now. More an 'it' than a person. That can happen to a soul consumed by envy and hatred."

"It is a demon!" said Saint Babukar. Then he pounded the table with an ebony fist. "And it is your enemy! It broke the Straight Road—your only way into the world. Think if it had destroyed it all!"

"Yes," said Nicholas. "You would have been shut out of the world forever, Klaus."

Klaus sat back and pondered the enormity of what this demon had almost accomplished. No more Christmas Eve deliveries. Ever. Everything that Castle Noël and the True North—and Anna and the Eight Flyers and Klaus himself—stood for, wiped out.

"Poor Rolf Eckhof," Anna said for the second time in her life. "It will be ages before he can be healed."

At that moment Saint Farouk hurried in and took his place at the table with a worried expression on his face. "Well, well," he said. "I have done all I can for poor Dasher."

"Will he be all right?" Klaus asked anxiously.

"His leg will mend, surely," Farouk said. "But I cannot recall him from the dreadful place his soul walks. He was in that terrible fog so long." He shook his head sadly.

"I thought those who Tarry could not be harmed," Klaus said.

Anna held up her damaged arm. "Apparently we can," she said ruefully.

"We are swimming in uncharted waters, I'm afraid," Saint Nicholas said.

They all looked at each other around the table. No one had an answer to what was happening.

"But one thing is certain," Nicholas continued. "The demon is bent on your destruction." He spread his hands on the table. "Indeed, that is all its life is now, I suspect: an unquenchable desire to make everyone as miserable as it is." He glanced at Anna. "It will strike at everyone and everything you love. It will strike at Christmas."

Elves repaired the Straight Road and the Green Council severed the tie that had tethered it to a fixed place in the Black Forest for so long. From that hour, its entire length was drawn up beyond the circles of the world. Now it touches the earth only in December and only where belief in Christmas is strongest. Wherever in the world the love of Christmas burns brightest, there the Straight Road will touch down. Meanwhile the demon that had been Rolf Eckhof roams the earth searching for it, and if it finds it, then the Road must be snatched up quickly or the demon will complete its work of destruction and shut Klaus out of the world forever.

Just before the Green Council departed, Saint Farouk took Klaus aside. "I do not know what will happen to Dasher," he said. "He is in a dark place. Maybe he will not find his way out."

"Oh," Klaus said. He could find no more words.

Farouk gripped his arm. "Your love for him is great," he said. "So have courage, my friend. There may be more for you to discover."

All through the autumn, Klaus tried hard to concentrate on organizing that year's Christmas preparations, but Anna could tell that his heart was not in it, and she knew the reason why: his deep worry over Dasher. Every day

Klaus spent hours sitting beside the reindeer where he lay, mute and unmoving, in his stable. There was a look of horror that never left Dasher's large brown eyes. "Where are you, old friend?" Klaus whispered into the reindeer's ear again and again. "Come back to us," he pleaded. But it was no use. Dasher did not come back.

And one day, just as the first snow fell in the pine forests of the True North and ice began to film the lake, Dasher closed his eyes, and Klaus felt him slipping even further away into darkness. From then on he would not leave him even for a moment. He forsook all pretense of preparing for that Christmas. He refused utterly, despite much urging, to name a new lead reindeer. And when Anna brought his meals to him at Dasher's side, he turned aside from them because for the first time in his life he had no appetite. Quietly, Anna took the reins of Christmas preparations. She organized the completion of that year's toy making and list checking. She studied the maps and charts for the annual deliveries, essential now that Dasher would not be leading the team. She gathered weather reports from around the world for Christmas Eve and even prepared to drive the sleigh. Klaus did not inquire about any of it. He had no care for anything but Dasher, whom he continually stroked and called by name: "Dasher. Dasher. Come back."

Late one weary December night, when Anna had joined Klaus in his vigil, she finally said to her husband, "Dasher Tarries for you. You must let him go."

"No!" Klaus cried, and clung to the reindeer.

"I also love him. He was mine before he was yours. But this life is not all, Klaus," Anna said. "Let him go to better pasturage."

Then Klaus knew that what his wife said was true. And so he whispered in Dasher's ear, "Great heart, I speak to you spirit to spirit. Your work here is done. You need no longer Tarry. Go in peace." And he released his hold on the beast.

At this Dasher opened his eyes, and the horror left them, replaced by a solemn joy. He lifted his great antlered head a little and looked at Anna and then at Klaus. "Be of good cheer!" he said to them. And died.

Klaus and Anna clung to each other and wept because they knew how much they would miss their friend and could only guess how long they would be parted from him. Then, arm in arm—Anna's good arm, of course—they walked out into what was left of the night. They were quiet, as one is after a momentous event, and took comfort in each other's silence.

A large full December moon hung in the velvet sky. The night was chilly, but not too cold as long as they clung to each other. They drifted past the castle, down to the lake, shining like a sheet of silver beneath the moon.

"Remember when you made me build him a house?" Klaus asked. "And it was really for you?"

"And remember how he wouldn't step one hoof into it?" Anna replied.

In spite of themselves, they chuckled at the good memory of their friend. And Anna observed that though Klaus was sad, a sweet acceptance had come to him. And by that she knew that he would heal and be whole again.

But down by the lake, something was stirring. It stepped out from the shadow of a tree into the full moonlight. Klaus and Anna stood transfixed. It used a little hoof to break the thin ice at the lake's edge and bent down to drink. Then it raised its head and looked straight at Anna and Klaus. It was smaller than the beasts they were accustomed to, but it was, without question, a reindeer. And from its tail to the very tip of its nose, which was glistening in the moonlight, it was bright scarlet red.

"Be of good cheer!" it called happily to Saint Anna and Saint Klaus.

CHAPTER SEVEN

Ranulf and the Demon

The Eight Flyers were stamping the ground, blowing steam, ready to depart for their long Christmas Eve flight. From the sleigh Klaus looked up to the front of the line. It was strange to see the small scarlet reindeer hitched beside Dancer in the lead traces. His scant spread of antlers scarcely came to the larger reindeer's shoulder. Could this jolly little fellow really take Dasher's place? Klaus swallowed hard. He missed seeing his steady, greathearted friend leading the team.

The moment of Dasher's passing was etched into his heart. So, too, were his last words: "Be of good cheer!"

Those had also been the first words the scarlet reindeer had said when he and Anna first glimpsed him by the lake in the moonlight later the same night. "Be of good cheer!" he had said. His voice was light and clear and seemed on the verge of bubbling over with mirth. "You know you will see your beloved again."

"Not for a long time," Klaus had replied sadly.

The little reindeer had come and rubbed against him for comfort. "That will make the meeting all the merrier," he said, "just as when you and Anna see each other again after a long Christmas Eve. My name is Ranulf. I have been sent to help. May I?" Klaus heard in Ranulf's question the echo of what he himself had said to those who had suffered losses from the Black Death so many years before; of what the Elves had asked to do on his and Anna's first day in the True North; and what Anna herself had done by establishing the vital institutions of the True North. *Helping is Magic*, he thought; *and Magic is really just a kind of helping*. He looked into the little reindeer's eyes, which were a remarkable emerald green, and saw behind them an outsized soul. "You are most welcome," he said.

At that, Ranulf had been so pleased that he leapt thirty

feet into the air and flew three times around Castle Noël, barrel-rolling and doing backflips all along the way. "Thank yoooouuuu!" he called out.

Klaus gazed up in astonishment. "I hope he doesn't do that when he's hitched to the sleigh," he said.

And Anna had replied, "I like him. He's my favorite color!"

Everyone had warmed to Ranulf's high spirits. It was almost as if he had come to help them through their grief at losing Dasher, and to cope with their dread of the demon who had struck him down. He exulted in fun and had immediately introduced new winter sports to the True North. Klaus had gasped when he first saw Ranulf skid gracefully across the frozen lake by Castle Noël. "It's called hoof skating!" he had called out. "Why not try it?" Soon all the reindeer were racing each other across the ice and dividing into teams to play ice hockey.

In the end, Klaus had had to be a bit stern: "We all have work to do if we're to make this year's deliveries! And besides, I don't want anyone breaking a leg! Ranulf, no more of these reindeer games until after Christmas!"

"Right, boss!" Ranulf had said cheerfully and led the way off the ice.

Now it was Christmas Eve and all were ready to depart.

Klaus stood up in the sleigh. It was time to find out if the red acrobat could lead the team. "On, Ranulf!" he cried. "And no barrel-rolling, please!"

The sleigh bowled down the thoroughfare of ice away from Castle Noël, silhouetted against the purple and gold of a True North sunset. Ranulf took two strides for every one of Dancer's, but he never tired. And the team followed well. They entered the Straight Road, which opened up suddenly before them as usual, and sped through the clouds down its length. Klaus had no idea where it would touch the earth, only that it would be where the love of Christmas burned brightest.

"Time Stop!" commanded Klaus halfway down the Straight Road. *And may Chronolepsy stop the demon, too*, Klaus fervently hoped.

And at first it looked as though it had. The Road shot to the ground. The two silver pots with their variegated holly bushes appeared like sentinels and anchored its entrance into the world. Klaus peered around, scanning the horizon on all sides for any sign of grayness. But there was nothing to see but the sunset winking through some snow-clad trees. Klaus allowed himself to relax a little. Chronolepsy had worked. He pulled out some maps and a compass to orient himself and began to think of his lists and deliveries.

But a sudden feeling of dread made him look up sharply. The demon was there. It had rushed to them with silent, deadly speed from wherever in the world it had been lurking. Klaus's heart sank. Chronolepsy had not even slowed it down. There it crouched, just beyond the foot of the Road, a ghastly, writhing menace. "Hold!" he called to his team, and they trotted to a halt. All was still for a moment. No one moved a muscle.

Then the demon let out a terrible moan. It was low at first, almost a whimper. But it soon grew to a mighty, agonizing din—like all the despairing souls of the world crying together. The reindeer fell to their knees and hung their antlered heads. This was simply too much for them. Their sight and hearing fled, and paralyzing horror crept into their hearts. With a malicious gurgle—almost a spiteful laugh—the cloud leapt onto the Road and began to melt it away like acid. Klaus jumped from his sleigh in a panic. If he did not act fast, all his reindeer would fall into the same black despair that had taken Dasher. And he would lose his tie to the earth. Forever.

He was about to make a desperate charge at the cloud when he heard a voice say, "Loose me." It was said with such calm command that at first Klaus was confused. *Surely that is Dasher's voice*, he thought. Then he saw that one reindeer had not fallen to its knees, nor hung its head. Little Ranulf stood upright and resolute, neither deaf nor blind. He glowered at the cloud, his green eyes blazing. "This Christmas Eve fog is for me. Loose me." Without a word, Klaus unhitched the reindeer. "Thanks, boss!" Ranulf piped in his normal, carefree voice and bugled his shrill little bugle. It rang out clear as a bell and cut off the demon's moan.

Then, still bugling, he stampeded into the grayness.

For a moment the little reindeer was completely hidden inside the awful, dreary mass, and Klaus could see nothing of the titanic struggle going on inside. Then the cloud shuddered and boiled with rage, and he caught a glimpse of Ranulf tossing his head again and again. *Why, he's pronging it with his antlers*, Klaus thought. *Sensible plan!*

But suddenly the cloud grew dark as night. Lightning flickered around its edges and stabbed into its interior. *Oh no*, thought Klaus, *he'll be killed!* He ran toward the fight, but then he heard Ranulf's sharp bugle again. A moment later the demon howled in pain and rage, lost its nerve, and fled into the sky. "Well done, Ranulf!" Klaus cried.

"Not done yet, boss!" Ranulf called. "Back in a minute!" And he rocketed into the air after the demon.

There followed one of the most epic aerial battles in all

of history—and none to see it except Klaus and the other seven Flyers, who began to revive as soon as the cloud was driven from the Road. Ranulf caught up with the fog in a scarlet flash. He bugled and pronged it again. The demon shrieked and streaked away at blinding speed, trying to get away from the searing pain of that agonizing sound and those sharp little antlers. But it could not. Wherever it zigged, Ranulf zigged. Wherever it zagged, Ranulf zagged and pronged again.

All of the other reindeer laughed and called his name: "Ranulf! Ranulf!" In response, Ranulf did a cartwheel in the sky. "It's called sky hoofing!" he called out. "Try it sometime!"

"Look out!" Klaus yelled in alarm. For the demon was now on the attack. It concentrated all the hatred and envy and desolation it could muster and charged the little reindeer from behind. If it had not put all its malevolence into that final, ultimate strike, it might have saved itself. But Ranulf turned in a flash and lowered his head and took the full force of the demon's charge. His antlers bit deep into the very heart of the cloud. A scream such as no one there had ever heard before, even in their nightmares, rent the air, and the cloud looked for a moment as if it would come apart in tatters. But then it pulled itself together and disappeared in an instant over the distant horizon. A moment later a flash of sheet lightning and a low rumble of thunder came from where it had fled.

Ranulf landed lightly beside Klaus. "You . . . see," he panted, "all those . . . reindeer games . . . paid off!"

From that day, the demon that had been Rolf Eckhof hated and feared Ranulf above all persons, and where the little reindeer is, he will not come. That is why, at the conclusion of each Christmas Eve, Ranulf stands guard at the bottom of the Straight Road until all of the other reindeer and Klaus have traveled safely up its length. He protects the precious link to the True North right up to the moment it is drawn safely up out of the world. And later Anna stitched a great work of art called *The Battle of Ranulf and the Demon*, which hangs in the Reception Hall of Castle Noël to this day.

Incidentally, the demon now loathes two colors, especially when they appear together: red—for Ranulf's remarkable coat—and green—for his piercing emerald eyes. And the sound of Ranulf's high-pitched bugle it cannot abide. So I advise you: Should you happen upon an evil cloud-demon, show it Christmas colors and bugle like a small scarlet reindeer, and you should be proof against it.

And now I have come almost to the end of my brief biography. All during that long Christmas Eve, Klaus flew over the continents of the earth and worked his age-old Magic, delivering toys to children in many lands, spreading happiness and hope with each gift—as he had always done. And many times in that enchanted night, Klaus laughed out loud, thinking of Ranulf's great victory over the demon—and for the sheer joy of making Christmas. "Ho, ho, ho!" he laughed. "Ho, ho, ho!" And each peal of laughter floated down from the sky onto the sleeping houses below like a benediction.

But, Esteemed Reader, will it always be so? Will Klaus always come into the world at Christmas?

Alas! Too few are now the places where the Straight Road may find purchase on the earth. For, as Saint Nicholas predicted, the demon has struck at Christmas, and struck hard. Unable to come at Klaus himself, it has assaulted humanity. Hundreds of years of simple gifts freely given out of the fondness and mirth in Klaus's soul, gradually at first, and then more rapidly, have turned into a frenzy of commerce and competition, until many in the world grow heartsick as Christmas approaches. And that is the demon's work.

Love for Klaus begins to wane. So, too, does understanding of what he really means: hearts knit together, belief in happiness just for itself and in the joy of causing it without judgment or profit, and, above all, hope: hope that in a cold time life will come again. And as the love of Christmas diminishes, the demon that was Rolf Eckhof grows steadily more potent as he haunts the world. He spreads his gloom wherever he can. His grayness enters hearts and they falter and lose their way.

And now we come to the heart of the matter and to the reason for *The Green Book*. Do not imagine this copy arrived in your hands by chance. It was made for you.

If you would fight the demon, tell people this true account of Klaus, of his youth as a wood carver and of his goodness to the people of his village. Spread the word about Anna and greathearted Dasher and the Green Council, about the splendors of the True North and what is done there. Drink a mug of peppermint hot chocolate with a friend and explain Chronolepsy and the Maya Principle and the Great Pact. Tell your family of the merry antics of Ranulf the Red Reindeer.

Like Klaus himself, you, Reader, can kindle Belief again. The original *Green Book* resides in the Father Goswin Library, an annex of Castle Noël. It is gone from the world and cannot be shown there again. And that is a good thing. The cynical world does not need more pale and weary proofs! It needs vibrant and vivid Belief in things it cannot see. Only that will keep the tie with the Straight Road strong so that Klaus may do his work.

And what is his work? Only healing the world of its hopelessness. Only curing it of its grayness. Only year by year helping the world remember that it has a heart.

And so, Dear Reader, I bid you, this year, and every year, the very merriest of Merry Christmases. And I entreat you: Spread the word!

Dunstan Wyatt

The Word

And so I finished Professor Wyatt's biography of Klaus. Before I fell asleep that December night, I looked again through the rest of the book. It all made sense now: the beautiful engravings, the flight charts and maps, the production figures and graphs, the Great Pact with its red wax seal. I thought about how Professor Wyatt and Ranulf must have meant for the book to fall from the sleigh as it sped up the Straight Road. And the Road must have touched the earth where it did because . . . well, because of me. Because

I believe in Christmas. Yes. I do. And now I knew why that was so important. And now, so do you. We all have to decide: Are we with Rolf Eckhof, or are we with Klaus?

When I woke up the next morning, stiff from sleeping all night in a desk chair, I was glad it was a Saturday. That meant nobody had to rush off to do anything in particular. I checked to see that everyone was still in the house. They were. My wife was already at her desk, paying bills. One boy was making French toast in the kitchen; the other was still snoring lightly in his bed. I woke that boy, gathered the wife into the kitchen, and asked the other boy to make enough French toast for everyone. I told them I had something to say, and that it might take a while.

"And, son," I said, "record me, will you? Because what I'm about to tell you is Important."

My wife sighed. "I can hear the capital 'I' in that last word. I'll make coffee."

"Right," said the boy and got the equipment he used with his band.

When everyone had settled, I looked at them one by one around the kitchen table. I took a deep breath.

And then I told them everything. Everything that had happened to me the day before. Every word of Klaus's biography, which, as Professor Wyatt had promised, I remembered with ease. When I got to the part about Klaus meeting Kelzang on his first Chronoleptic Christmas Eve flight, one boy mused, "They must have been at Potala Palace in Lhasa."

"Where is that?" I said.

"Tibet. Kelzang Gyatso was the Seventh Dalai Lama."

"From 1708 to 1757," the other boy volunteered. "Everyone knows that. Keep going. This is pretty interesting."

And I did. I kept going until I had recited the entire book, finishing sometime in the afternoon. "'Spread the word,'" I concluded. "That's what Professor Wyatt said we have to do."

There was silence for a moment around the sofas in the family room to which we had drifted sometime during my recitation. Then:

"Wow," one boy said.

The other boy said, "Let me support that comment: wow."

Another moment of silence.

"It really is the best story you've ever told us," my wife said.

"Thank you," I said, gratified. Then, "Wait, no. This isn't a story. Haven't you been listening? This really happened. This is all true." No one said anything. "You believe me, don't you?" I asked. My wife got that patient look on her face. The boys exchanged glances. "Wait," I said. I ran down to the study and came back with a piece of paper and gave it to my wife. "There. That's the note Professor Wyatt left when he took *The Green Book*. See?"

She studied it, passed it wordlessly to one boy. He looked it over and said, "It's in your handwriting, Dad."

I snatched it back. "No, it isn't," I said, though, upon examination, it did look a lot like my handwriting—an uncanny parallel I hadn't noticed before. I could see how they might make a mistake. "Well then, what about my being able to recite from *The Green Book* without correcting myself—or even pausing?" I asked.

"It was fantastic!" the boy said, checking his recording equipment. "I'm glad we got it down."

"You really are a born storyteller," my wife said, smiling. "How do you come up with it all? *The Green Book*. I like it."

I was flabbergasted. They didn't believe me. Was Rolf Eckhof at work even in my own family? "Wait, wait," I said. "What about how I was stuck in the snow up on the mountain? How do you explain that I got home?"

My wife got a funny sort of worried look on her face. She excused herself for a moment and came back with her own piece of paper. "This is the notification from the tow-truck driver that he submitted his bill to our insurance company." She handed me the email. "For pulling you out of the snow last night."

I stared at the paper. I was in shock. "I'm telling you, cross my heart and hope to never celebrate Christmas again, everything I've told you is true," I said.

The boys were looking a little uncomfortable. My wife frowned. "Honestly, dear, why do you have to take everything so far? We've said we like your story."

"But it isn't a story," I protested weakly.

"I'm sure you boys have lots to do on a Saturday," my wife said.

"Right," said one.

"Thanks for the great story, Dad!" said the other.

"I told you, it isn't . . ." But they were gone. I looked at the paper again. "There was no tow truck," I said.

"Oh, honestly," said my wife. "The evidence is staring you in the face."

The next couple of weeks were the most miserable I can remember. I would try to talk to my family about my experience, try to persuade them about Klaus and the True North, and at first they were patient, but before long they just didn't want to hear about it anymore. I didn't mention it to anyone else. And as the bright memory of that day in the mountains began to recede into the past, it faded and got muddled. Had I really seen an Elevated Spirit? Had I really heard a reindeer talk? It had all seemed so real, but maybe it wasn't. On one subject, however, I was clear. Or mostly. There had been no tow truck. How could I have forgotten a whole tow truck? After a week my mind started to lose the words of *The Green Book*. It was recorded, of course, but I found I didn't want to go back and listen to it.

Usually in December, I attack Christmas tasks with a kind of manic glee. This year I found I just wasn't up to it. I asked the boys to put up the Christmas lights. I found it hard to shop for presents. The heart had gone out of the holidays, and everything around me began to look a little . . . gray.

But on Christmas Eve, I tried to pull myself together. I figured I owed it to my family. It had snowed a couple of days before, and the world was fresh and white again. I bundled up and went for a late afternoon walk in the neighborhood, just to try to straighten myself out. As I trudged along, I brooded on all that had happened, and for some reason I began thinking about it in a new way: Klaus in his village, figuring out how to help his mourning neighbors and finding joy in it. Anna and then Dasher bringing hope to Klaus when he despaired of making his Christmas Eve deliveries. And then suddenly, easily, like a whisper in the

December air, a great truth breathed gently into me and blew away the gray: If the True North and Castle Noël and Anna's maple sugar cookies were made up, then the hope and joy they represented were not. And if I had concocted the whole story because I wanted so fervently to believe in Christmas Magic, well, Christmas was magic enough all on its own. It didn't need my story. Hope and joy. They were enough to live a life on.

As I walked back home, the sun began to set. On the houses I passed, Christmas lights started to wink on. In the east, Jupiter was rising above the mountains. My spirits lifted. I sang a carol softly to myself: "God rest ye merry, gentlemen. Let nothing you dismay." I was happy about Christmas again.

In fact I was so happy that as I plodded up our steep driveway and admired the lights the boys had put up—we favor the big colored bulbs—I didn't really notice a sharp spicy scent in the air. And when I saw one boy at the side of the house scanning the horizon in high excitement, I didn't at first understand he was looking for me.

But he was. "Dad!" he shouted. "Thank goodness you're home! Come into the backyard!" And then, when I didn't actually run, he shouted, "Hurry! Come on!" and disappeared around the corner of the house.

That's when I registered the scent in the air. *Oh my*, I thought, and then, *Could it be?* I wondered. I sprinted into the backyard.

There was my wife bundled up in a quilt and pack boots as though she had just come out from a long winter's nap. *How like Anna she looks!* I suddenly thought. And there were the boys, underdressed for the cold as usual. And all three were staring with shining eyes.

What were they staring at? Why, at two silver pots, each engraved with a star and a reindeer rampant. And at two variegated holly bushes in silver pots from which the sweet scent of peppermint was perfuming the frosty air. And at the new snow in our backyard, all patterned and churned with the hoof marks of reindeer and the track of a sleigh taking off into the Christmas Eve sky.

Oh, I must tell you: When we called our insurance company after Christmas, they knew nothing about any tow truck.

Spread the word.

ABOUT THE AUTHOR

TIM SLOVER is a writer and professor of theater at the University of Utah. His plays have been produced off-Broadway and in theaters throughout the United States and in London, where he spends part of each year. His wife, usefully, is a marriage and family therapist, and their two sons were the original audience for *The Christmas Chronicles*. For the purposes of yuletide decorating, each Christmas Slover continues to cut a few pine boughs at an undisclosed location.

ABOUT THE TYPE

This book was set in Goudy, a typeface designed by Frederic William Goudy (1865–1947). Goudy began his career as a bookkeeper, but devoted the rest of his life to the pursuit of "recognized quality" in a printing type.

Goudy was produced in 1914 and was an instant bestseller for the foundry. It has generous curves and smooth, even color. It is regarded as one of Goudy's finest achievements.